ADVANCE PRAISE FOR *PERIPHERAL VISIONS AND OTHER STORIES*

"A memorable cast of characters engaged in a beguiling group of situations...I recommend *Peripheral Visions and Other Stories* highly." **Hal Blythe, Co-Director, Teaching & Learning Center, Eastern Kentucky University**

"Nancy Christie's stories open up worlds that exist just off to the side of the ordinary one we all inhabit, reinvigorating the reader's senses by revealing what we often don't see in the peripheries of our vision." **Christopher Barzak, author of Wonders of the Invisible World**

"Some of the best of modern short story fiction.... She engages the reader from the start and whether with gentle humour or deep sadness, imbues her stories with emotion. This collection provides a thoroughly satisfying read." **Rosemary J. Kind, Managing Director, Alfie Dog Fiction**

"Wonderful short stories with believable characters finding meaning in the stuff of real life—broken relationships, difficult situations, human longings. I highly recommend this book." **John Feister, Editor in Chief, St. Anthony Messenger**

"Nancy Christie's stories are the dichotomy of youth and age, of experience and memory, of harmony and friction, of life and death. They are old relations. To read *Peripheral Visions and*

Other Stories is to carefully sort through a found box of dusty photographs, to answer old questions and discover new ones. This book brings you closer to your own family." **Lee L. Krecklow, author of *The Expanse Between***

"Wonderful delights of the strange and the sadly familiar. ... a fun read from this promising writer." **Michael M. Pacheco, author of *Of Angels, Demons and Chopped Chorizo***

"The stories in Nancy Christie's *Peripheral Visions* ... are fictions that focus on dramatic moments and emotions rather than earth-shattering conflicts, and as such, they are always appealing, and more than a little heartbreaking." **Clifford Garstang, author of *In an Uncharted Country* and *What the Zhang Boys Know* (winner of the 2013 Library of Virginia Award for Fiction), and editor of *Everywhere Stories: Short Fiction from a Small Planet***

"Nancy Christie masterfully spins tales of ordinary people confronted with the extraordinary circumstances of modern life, and she does so with a warmth that belies the sometimes cold reality of lives at a crossroads and people on the brink." **Dean Johnson, author of *Californium* and *Delicate Men: Stories***

"Reading Nancy Christie's collection is like spending time in a town inhabited by familiar-feeling residents who first pique your curiosity then draw you into their lives... we get to know characters who seem as though they could be our neighbors, coworkers, relatives and friends, facing challenges that elicit our empathy and reveal facets of our shared humanity." **Soramimi Hanarejima, author of *Visits to the Confabulatorium***

Peripheral Visions and Other Stories

By

Nancy Christie

PERIPHERAL VISIONS AND OTHER STORIES
Nancy Christie
Copyright © 2020 Nancy Christie

All rights reserved. Printed in the United States of America. No part of this book may be used or reproduced in any manner whatsoever without written permission except in the case of brief quotations embodied in critical articles or reviews.

The following stories have been published in the following journals:

"Remember Mama — *Talking River*
"When Ann Calls" — *Wild Violet*
"Ice Cream Sunday" — *Fiction 365*
"Memories of Music" — *St. Anthony Messenger*
"The Accident" — *Alfie Dog*
"Aunt Aggie and the Makeup Lady" — *The Chaffin Journal*
"Accidents Will Happen" — *Streetlight Magazine*
"Boxing Life" — *Two Cities Review*
"Going Home" — *One Person's Trash*
"Lost and Found"— *Ariel Chart*

Attention schools and businesses: for discounted copies on large orders, please contact the publisher directly.

For information contact:
Unsolicited Press
Portland, Oregon
www.unsolicitedpress.com
orders@unsolicitedpress.com
619-354-8005

Editor: Analieze Cervantes
Cover Design: Kathryn Gerhardt

ISBN: 978-1-950730-40-7

Table of Contents

AUNT AGGIE AND THE MAKE-UP LADY	1
LOST AND FOUND	13
REMEMBER MAMA	18
WHEN ANN CALLS	28
THE ACCIDENT	33
'TIL DEATH DO US PART	42
LITTLE BOY FOUND	53
I REMEMBER....	59
ICE CREAM SUNDAY	70
PANDORA'S BOX	76
LUCINDA AND THE CHRISTMAS LIST	93
BOXING LIFE	108

THE FLOWERBED	114
BURNING BRUSHES	125
MEMORIES OF MUSIC	131
AFTER THE STORM	139
GOING HOME	143
ACCIDENTS WILL HAPPEN	151
STARTING TO SURFACE	155
PERIPHERAL VISIONS	163

PERIPHERAL VISIONS AND OTHER STORIES

AUNT AGGIE AND THE MAKE-UP LADY

When Billy said he repaired the gutters, I should never have believed him. That was my first mistake.

If I had checked them myself, I would have realized the job had to be done all over again—but the right way this time. Then, the three-day rain wouldn't have loosened them from the roof. And I would have been inside the house instead of dangling from an aluminum piece ten feet off the ground, and Aunt Aggie and the make-up lady would never have had their fateful meeting.

Aunt Aggie wasn't even my aunt but somehow, during the division of marital property, I ended up with her. She was married to Billy's father's brother, and therefore, didn't even have a blood claim to the family, but she always liked Billy and kind of adopted us as her own children, since she didn't have any of her own.

Everybody liked Billy. That was the problem. Billy was a real likable devil, and women were always falling for his charm and curly hair and big blue eyes. Even when he left them crying over the results of their pregnancy tests, they still wanted him to come back.

I can't fault the women. Hell, I knew what he was like and I *still* married him. But after the last time, I just had to draw the line. It was all getting too ridiculous.

Billy was a truck driver and was due to take a load of beef on a two-week haul across the country. That was his story. But when his girlfriend in Tucson called to ask if he'd left yet, I knew I'd had enough—especially when the fourteen-day trip turned into sixteen months.

So, we split up, and Billy got the tractor-trailer rig, and I got the house and two kids and the mortgage. And Aunt Aggie.

I don't mind about Aunt Aggie—not really. It took me some time to get used to her appearance—the frizzy dyed red hair, the three-inch coat of mascara on her stubby lashes, the jangly assortment of pins, necklaces, and bracelets she wore from early in the morning to late at night. I often suspected she wore the jewelry to bed, but never wanted to know badly enough to voluntarily enter her bedroom. I needed at least an eight-hour break each day from Aggie and her peculiarities.

Most of the year, Aunt Aggie lived in a small trailer court just outside Vegas, along with about a dozen or so other old people. But every now and then, the urge would come over her to visit her "family," and she would descend on us like a gambler's idea of Santa, with poker chips and paper umbrellas for the kids, and sample bottles of shampoo, soap, and sometimes even bath towels for me.

For an old lady, Aunt Aggie had very fast fingers.

In her defense, I must say that her visits never lasted very long, and she can be very entertaining, in a bizarre kind of way. She taught the children how to play poker and gin rummy, and only argued a little when I told her there would be no betting with their allowance.

"But, MaryLynn," she had said, when I removed the stacks of quarters, dimes, and nickels in front of her, "how can you expect the children to take the game seriously if they don't have anything to lose?"

"It's a game, for God's sakes," I had answered, shoving the coins back into the piggy banks she had robbed. "I don't want the children gambling."

"Life's a gamble," she had muttered, but brightened up when I offered to make cocoa and popcorn. Aunt Aggie liked to eat. I had headed off many a dispute by shoving assorted solids and liquids into her mouth, until she looked like a chubby chipmunk gorging before winter.

But anyway, I was telling you about the make-up lady. So here I was, hanging one-handed off the gutter, hollering for my son Matthew to come out and set the ladder back up. I had kicked it over when I reached a bit too far to hammer in that last nail. Then I heard the doorbell ring.

"Shit," and I let go of the edge and landed flat on my butt in the mud.

"I'll get it," I yelled to Aunt Aggie, without really believing she would pass up an opportunity to meet someone new. Aunt Aggie was a very sociable person. She never missed a chance to meet new acquaintances, even when they clearly didn't want to meet her.

By the time I had wiped the worst of the mud from the seat of my pants and got into the kitchen, Aunt Aggie was already in full conversational spate.

"And so I told my nephew I'd keep an eye on them while he's gone" (Aunt Aggie never believed me when I told her Billy and I were divorced) "so here I am. And here's MaryLynn!" She waved her greasy fingers with a flourish as if she'd conjured me out of thin air. Obviously, the visitor had interrupted Aunt Aggie's breakfast, which started about nine in the morning and lasted until lunch.

"Can I help you?" I said, eyeing the woman. She didn't look like a social worker or a humane society investigator. I had met both their kinds when Matthew tied six piglets to the front of his wagon in an attempt to imitate the chariot race in *Ben Hur*.

It had been Aunt Aggie's idea for him to watch that movie. But I could never get her to admit to instigating the pig participation.

"Hi," the woman said brightly. "My name is Sue Ann Burton and I wanted to stop by and introduce myself to the ladies of the family."

At this point, Aunt Aggie casually removed her upper dentures and dropped them into a nearby glass of water. Sue Ann's eyes widened but she went gamely on.

"I offer the 'Lovely Lady' line of cosmetics and, to introduce them to you, I would like to give you a complimentary make-up demonstration. It will only take about fifteen minutes. Where would you like to sit?"

She was good, I'll give her that. Aunt Aggie had made many people lose track of their thoughts, not to mention their minds, but Sue Ann wasn't about to give up a chance at a sale.

"This really isn't a good time," I started but Aunt Aggie cut me off at the pass.

"Oh, let's do it, MaryLynn. It'll be fun!"

Aunt Aggie thought everything was fun. If she had lived during the French Revolution, she would have been one of those village women gathered at the foot of the guillotine. Except she would have been eating, not knitting. And no doubt betting on the number of heads that would roll in a given time.

In the meantime, Sue Ann was laying out her little bottles and jars, shoving aside the bills, coupons, and lottery tickets littering the table.

"Let me tell you about our products," she continued, pushing brochures in front of both of us. "All of our make-up items are all natural, hypo-allergenic and made from plant extracts. And none of them are tested on animals. 'Lovely Lady' doesn't believe in animal testing."

"Mamma!" Little Becky came screeching into the kitchen, skidding past Sue Ann, and grabbing hold of my arm. "You have to stop Matt! He's feeding crayons to Bozo!"

"Matthew! You stop that right now!" I leaned out the window, trying to spot my son and the long-suffering dog. Poor Bozo. He was the nicest pet we'd ever had—part Labrador and part some other unidentifiable breed—but he didn't have enough brains to move away from danger.

"Ahhh, Mom," and my son appeared under the windowsill, crayon pieces clutched in his grubby hands. "I just wanted to see if Bozo would poop in color."

"Never mind Bozo's poop. You leave him alone!" and I banged down the window. When I turned back to the table, Sue Ann was staring at me, open-mouthed. "Sorry," I said. "Unlike 'Lovely Lady,' I'm afraid my son does believe in animal testing. But I'm trying to break him of that," and I picked up the sample of "Starry Night" night cream. "Now where were we?"

"Uh, yes," and, with a little mental effort, Sue Ann got back into the swing. "Now, which of you would like to go first?" and she looked at me hopefully. It would take more than a quarter of an hour to improve Aunt Aggie's looks. It would probably take at least that long to remove the layers of makeup she was already wearing.

"Me! Me!" Aunt Aggie squealed, like a kid in a toy shop.

Resignedly, Sue Ann slipped a smock around Aunt Aggie's wrinkled neck, and pulled some tissues from her bag.

"We'll start with a cleansing lotion," she said as she carefully she began wiping the four pounds of rouge from Aunt Aggie's wrinkled cheeks. Aunt Aggie liked wearing lots of rouge—the redder, the better. "This cleansing lotion is made from mint and chamomile leaves, carefully crushed and combined with a milk base. Remember, all natural products," she added.

"All natural," Aunt Aggie mused, catching some of the tissue in her mouth by accident. She spit it out and continued. "No animal testing, right?"

I could see that Aunt Aggie had something in her mind and from experience, I knew it would be off-beat.

"That's right," Sue Ann agreed heartily. "We don't want to see animals suffer just so we can look beautiful, do we?"

"But you smashed plants to make this," Aunt Aggie objected.

"Well, yes, but plants have no feelings," Sue Ann said, bewildered by the line the conversation was taking. In the meantime, my eyes caught the headline in the trashy weekly on the table—"Plant Protection Group Seeks End to Violence."

"But in *Today's Top Tales*," and Aunt Aggie brandished the tabloid—her favorite reading material—in Sue Ann's face, "it says that all plants and flowers and trees have feelings. That's why they grow better when you talk nice to them. Isn't that right, MaryLynn? Why, your African violet got huge, and all I did was talk to it night and day!"

Privately, I always thought it was the effect of all that carbon dioxide hitting the leaves, but I kept my mouth shut. For every hour Aunt Aggie spent conversing with my flowers, I gained sixty minutes of peace and quiet.

"So, if you crushed the plants to make the cream, you must have hurt them. Right?" she finished triumphantly.

"Well, I'm sure it was fast and they didn't suffer," Sue Ann said helplessly, trying to keep in mind the old rule that the customer is always right.

Poor Sue Ann was beginning to look a little frayed around the edges, like a shirt that had gone through the wringer one too many times. But like a trouper, she bit her lip and kept on going, rubbing the rest of the lotion from Aunt Aggie's face. I didn't even hold it against her that she used a little more force than was necessary.

But by the time she was through, she had regained some measure of self-control, and heroically continued with the demonstration.

"Now, we'll apply some anti-wrinkle cream. This will reduce signs of aging by fifty percent." Tenderly, she smoothed the white cream onto the hills and valleys of Aunt Aggie's seventy-plus-year-old face.

"Now, how does that feel?" and she stood back a moment, giving Aunt Aggie a chance to look into the mirror she had so thoughtfully provided.

"I still have wrinkles," Aunt Aggie objected.

"Well, yes," Sue Ann said nervously. "But it takes time for the cream to make a difference."

"But you said fifty percent." Aunt Aggie's mind was like a steel trap. When she got an idea in her head, she wasn't going to release it no matter what. "I don't think I look any better at all. And it's starting to itch," and she rubbed at her cheek with the back of her hand. A red spot appeared, and soon another showed up on her forehead.

"Perhaps you'd better wash it off," I suggested, as Aunt Aggie continued to rub at the new spots that were showing up remarkably fast. "She sometimes has reactions to certain things," I explained to Sue Ann, not bothering to add that Aunt Aggie was more likely to cause reactions than suffer from them.

"I'm terribly sorry." Poor Sue Ann was nearly in tears. "This has never happened before!"

"Don't worry," I soothed her, as Aunt Aggie hurried to the kitchen sink to wash the lotion from her face. "It wasn't your fault."

Aunt Aggie returned, her wrinkled face all restored back to its natural state, and ready for another go-around.

"Now what?" she asked brightly, and with a resigned sigh, Sue Ann opened another bottle.

"First, we'll smooth on a bit of 'Tighten Up' toner to close the pores." I resisted the urge to point out that it would take industrial equipment to close those openings. "Then, perhaps a light dusting of 'Rubies of the Nile' blush."

Carefully, she applied a bit of the rose-colored powder to Aunt Aggie's cheeks, where it immediately settled into all the creases.

"What about lipstick?" and Aunt Aggie pursed her lips, ready for the next stage.

By now, Sue Ann's shoulders had started to droop, and she looked as if she could do with a bit of "Tighten Up" toner herself.

"Lipstick, certainly," and she swiveled up a tube of "Egyptian Ochre" to apply to Aunt Aggie's mouth. "This formula is designed to stay on for a whole day, even through meals," obviously reciting another part of the company's spiel.

I wondered if they had ever tested its staying power on someone like Aunt Aggie, who only stopped eating to sleep—and maybe not even then, if the crumbs in the sheets were any indicator.

"I like lipstick," Aunt Aggie commented, as Sue Ann did her best to work with the moving mass of redness that was Aunt Aggie's mouth. "I think it makes you look younger. Don't you think so?" She craned her neck to look at me, causing Sue Ann to trace a bright red line from the corner of her mouth to her ear. She looked like a deranged clown.

Sue Ann bit her lip and a few tears slipped from her eyes. Grabbing a bottle of make-up remover, she hurriedly dumped some onto a tissue and tried rubbing the red line from Aunt Aggie's cheek. But it soon became apparent that the lipstick's staying power had not been exaggerated.

"Oh, Lord," and the tears began to fall in earnest. "I'm no good at this," Sue Ann wept, sniffling into the red-stained tissue. "I should never have tried selling cosmetics!"

"Now, just sit down and it'll all be okay." I pulled out a chair and practically pushed the poor woman into it. "And Aunt Aggie," noticing the tell-tale red spots beginning to make yet another appearance, "perhaps you'd better go wash your face again."

Once I got Sue Ann settled, I poured her a glass of water. "Just drink this," I said authoritatively. Between Billy and the kids and, of course, Aunt Aggie, I had a lot of experience with hysterics. "And don't let this little setback stop you from your new career. Why, with an attitude like that, I would never have had a second kid!" At this, Sue Ann gave me a half-way smile.

"Just take a little break and everything will look better in a minute." I pulled out a chair and sat across from her. "How long have you been doing this?" I asked curiously.

"You're my first client," Sue Ann said in between sniffs. "I got laid off from the factory and they made it sound so easy and the bills keep coming in and I don't know what to do! I'm such a failure!" and she started crying all over again.

"Well, what you're going to do is stop crying. Puffy eyes never sold any make-up," I said cheerfully. "As for being a failure, don't be ridiculous. Aunt Aggie just has that effect on people. Besides, how can you say you're no good when you just made" and I did a quick calculation of how much grocery money was in my wallet and how long the milk and bread could be made to last, "a twenty-dollar sale?"

"Really? You'll buy some make-up?" Poor Sue Ann's face glowed. "I don't know how to thank you!"

"It's nothing," and I slid the twenty out of my wallet. "But do me a favor, kid. Put this stuff away before Aunt Aggie wants a wax job."

Sue Ann giggled, and then starting loading her bottles and jars into the bag with more speed than professionalism. "But what will you buy?" she asked suddenly. "You haven't said what you want. Here's an order form" and she set it down in front of me.

I looked at the list. Day cream, night cream, blusher, mascara, lipstick, eye shadow—everything a woman could want to look good, assuming there was anyone around besides her kids who was going to be looking at her.

"Tell you what," I said, pushing the list back to Sue Ann. "You're the professional. I'll let you decide what I need."

Just then, Becky and Matthew came racing into the kitchen, with Bozo in hot pursuit. They careened off the table, scattering Sue Ann's belongings all over the top. One bottle of "Scarlet Sunset" nail polish rolled off the edge, and in a matter of seconds, there was a puddle of red on the floor.

Bozo stopped to sniff, dabbing his nose into the sticky mess, and then walked through it. I could follow his path by the red trail he left behind.

With speed born of experience, I mopped up the floor as best as I could while Sue Ann finished putting her items in the case. Then, she took another look at the order form.

"What you need," she repeated, and then checked off one of the boxes with resolution. "This will be perfect," she said with more assurance than she had shown so far.

"Your order will be in next week," and she set the paper down on top of the rest of the clutter on the table. Just then, we heard Aunt Aggie coming down the hall, and I winked at Sue Ann.

"You better beat it," I said solemnly, and she giggled, her good humor back in force.

"Thanks for everything," and she gave me a quick hug at the door. "I'll see you next week," and she made it down the porch steps just as Aunt Aggie came in for Stage Two.

"Where did she go? I wanted my nails done," she said disappointedly.

"Too late," I answered. "She can only do one manicure per home and Bozo beat you to it."

I walked back into the kitchen, curious to see what Sue Ann had checked off with such confidence.

The red mark was easy to spot. And I was right. Sue Ann did know what I needed: a three-month supply of "Stress Repair Formula," with a money-back guarantee.

PERIPHERAL VISIONS AND OTHER STORIES

LOST AND FOUND

Jesse had been collecting things for as long as he could remember. All kinds of things: a bit of dirty twine that once tied shut a bag of birdseed. A blue marble with a chip marring its perfect roundness. A rusty padlock with a key trapped inside.

He didn't know why he sought out these items, why they called to him amid the flotsam and jetsam that littered the city streets. Why the marble and not the bottle cap next to it? Why the twine and not the skein of faded red yarn? Why the padlock—no, that one was easy. People bought padlocks because they wanted to protect something.

Somewhere there was a box or a cupboard that contained a secret, a treasure, an *objet d'art* that needed to be secured and protected. But until the padlock was put back where it belonged, the terrible risk of loss existed.

The padlock with its key was the only item that Jesse carried with him all the time as he wandered the streets. The rest he kept hidden in a cardboard shoebox that once held "EZ-Strider Men's Brown Loafers, Size 12 Extra Wide Width" that he had pulled from the trashcan outside Aunt Martha's back door.

Not that she was his aunt. That was just what she had told him to call her when the Family Services lady left him there six months ago. Sometimes, the people said he could use "aunt" and "uncle." Other times, like at the last place, he had to be more formal: "Mr. and Mrs. Blackthorpe" or "Reverend and Mrs. Collier." Although when he was five and a half, there was a woman who said he could call her Annie.

"Just Annie," she had told him while she hung up his two pairs of jeans and one jacket, the one that was really too small but was all he had. "I'm pretty easy-going," she had continued, and he took her at her word.

Everybody did. Annie had bright blue eyes, a big smile that showed her small white teeth, red hair that she wore pulled back in a white-and-black checked scrunchy, and freckles. Lots of freckles. Freckles on her face. On her arms and legs. Even on the palms of her hands. One time he counted seventeen of them before he felt the sting of her flesh against his face. She had held her hand, for what seemed like forever, inches before his eyes, and he had just made it to the cluster at the base of her thumb before her hand came so close that it all blurred and then all he could think about was how important it was not to cry.

"I told you to empty your pockets before you put your filthy pants in the washer," she said, still smiling. "This is what happens when you forget," meting out one punishing blow for each of the eight items that she found in the bottom of the washer tub: a nail, a penny, a bottle cap, a blue jay's feather, a plastic spoon, a tiny screwdriver, a broken watchband, and half of a lottery ticket.

Once it was over, she made him retrieve each item from the chipped porcelain tub and throw them all away. At least, she thought they were thrown away. But later that night, after she fell asleep, he left the lumpy couch that served as his bed and dug through the greasy chicken bones and takeout containers in the trash bag until he found every one of them. He didn't know where else to keep them safe so he dug a hole in the dirt next to the garbage cans and hid them deep inside.

Jesse's plan was to retrieve them before he left Annie's house forever. He knew that someday he *would* leave or be taken away. But when that day came, the social worker picked him up at his school, not at Annie's house, and he was put in the back seat next to a bag with what little clothes he had and whisked away so fast he couldn't even ask to go back.

He never forgot about them though. He wrote down Annie's address on a scrap of paper and mentally promised all those lost items that he would come back and take them away. He still had that paper, even after four more moves, and it was now safely stored in his shoebox. But not at Aunt Martha's. After what happened at Annie's, he knew the danger of keeping special things at the places he stayed.

No, the box was around the corner and down the street, at the small playground next to the bar where Aunt Martha spent her Friday nights. Jesse had put the box inside a plastic store bag from Benny's Bargain Outlet and then, climbing the one lone maple tree that shaded the broken swing set, shoved it inside a hollowed-out opening in the trunk, hoping the squirrels wouldn't decide to investigate what was inside.

Then he kept adding to it what he had found, even though the box was starting to bulge on one side from all that he put in it.

But the padlock and key—no, that stayed with him, for reasons even he couldn't have explained if someone had asked. Not that anyone was *likely* to ask him about it—or anything else, for that matter. No one asked Jesse anything: not the teachers (when he showed up at school, which was rarely), not the social worker when she came to check up on him (which was rarer still), and certainly not Aunt Martha because half the time she didn't even know who he was.

"Billy? Frank? What's your name again?" waving the whiskey bottle at him as though to clear away the imaginary cobwebs that obscured her vision.

"Jesse," he would tell her, and then come closer so she could see him better. "My name is Jesse," and she would just grin, take another swig, and fall asleep, leaving him to forage for what food he could find before he went out on his nightly scavenger hunt.

It wasn't all that bad at Aunt Martha's, he decided, taking a bite out of his peanut butter sandwich after first inspecting the bread for signs of mold or ants. (Some days, he found both, but other days—"lucky days," he called them—the bread was relatively insect- and fungus-free.)

She didn't hit him. She didn't complain if he left stuff in his pockets. (Or maybe she didn't know. Most of the time, Jesse did the laundry at the Wash-O-Mat around the corner.) And there was usually something to eat. Some days, she would even take him with her to the Indian grocery store and let him buy anything that caught his eye as long as it was under three dollars and eligible for purchase with her food-stamp card: a jar of bitter gourd pickles, passion fruit juice, mango chutney.

It was at least better than others—definitely better than the Mr.-and-Mrs. Bad House. That's how he thought of it— the place that came with nightly visits from one or both of the two adults who were supposed to be caring for him. He would pretend to be sleeping, but that didn't help. If it hadn't been for the blood that had seeped from his pants onto the desk chair where his teacher spotted it, he might still be there.

If there were places he was at when he was even younger— before Annie's, before the institution—he didn't recall. And if he once had a home—a real home with a mother or father or maybe even both—his mind couldn't travel that long journey into the past. He tried. He would tightly close his eyes and pretend to be a toddler or a baby, and wait for something, a sound or smell or touch, that would open those long-closed doors.

But it didn't happen.

Instead, he wandered the streets, one hand wrapped firmly around the padlock and key, looking for a box of memories that he could once again safely secure against loss.

NANCY CHRISTIE

REMEMBER MAMA

"Maggie, where's my tea?"

Maggie set down the dishcloth and moved to answer her mother's call. The rest of the china, like so many other tasks half-completed, would have to wait.

"You had your tea already, Mama. Remember? I brought you a cup of tea and you finished it and said you didn't want any more."

But the old woman shook her head obstinately.

"No, I didn't. You never brought it. I've been waiting for hours," the now-familiar note of self-pity creeping into her voice, "and you never brought it to me."

Maggie smothered a sigh. There was no point in arguing with her mother. She could show her the cup she drank from and her mother still wouldn't remember.

Couldn't, Maggie corrected herself. Her mother *couldn't* remember. She had to keep reminding herself of that fact or the frustration would soon grow too strong to handle.

"Where is—where is—" Her mother struggled for a name and then gave up. "Where did he go?"

"Paul"—the name emphasized just a bit, "had to go away on a business trip. To California. I told you all about it, Mama. Remember?"

Paul, who had shown infinite patience and tenderness with his mother-in-law. He pretended everything was normal and persisted in carrying on one-sided conversations with her about the weather, current events, upcoming plans for the weekend.

But lately, her mother couldn't even remember his name.

"Oh, yes, now I remember." But her mother's voice held no conviction. "It just slipped my mind for a moment." She looked at her daughter, obviously hoping that the excuse would be accepted.

Maggie nodded her head, joining her mother in the delusion. "Mama's poor memory"—how often she and her father had teased her mother about her inability to recall names, dates, places. It had been humorous once, but no longer. Now it was a tragic reality.

After Maggie's father had died, her mother had become distracted and forgetful, and initially Maggie put much of the blame on grief. But even sorrow, she was finally forced to admit, couldn't wreak such havoc on a person's mental abilities. Even grief couldn't keep you from recalling where you lived, where you were going, whether or not you'd eaten or slept or changed your clothes. Only sickness could do that.

Remembering this, Maggie asked with more patience, "Do you want another cup of tea now, Mama?" as she straightened the soft throw across her mother's narrow, blue-veined feet. Maggie recalled watching her mother knit the soft mix of blue and cream and orchid yarns during the long nights in the hospital, the clicking sound of the needles a counterpoint to the noise of the respirator that filled her father's lungs with air.

Someday, she would think, she would have to ask her mother to show her how to knit like that.

But there was never a free moment to learn. And now, her mother couldn't even tie her own shoes.

"No, I'm not thirsty anymore. But I am hungry, Maggie. How soon is dinner?"

"Not for a long time, Mama. We just had lunch." Her mother frowned, and Maggie knew she didn't recall the omelet filled with cheese and herbs that her daughter had carefully prepared just half an hour ago. She went on quickly.

"I thought I'd make a roast for dinner, with new potatoes and green beans with dill. Would you like that for dinner, Mama?" knowing the question was pointless even as it was asked. No matter what her mother's initial response was, she was certain to change her mind by the time the food was ready. But Maggie had to keep the fiction alive that her mother's opinions and desires counted for something, as inconsistent as they were.

Her mother was silent for a moment, considering, and then shook her head. "I don't like beans—they've got strings. Why can't we have carrots instead?"

Maggie smiled. "Okay, Mama, I'll make carrots. Carrots in honey sauce, like you used to do. Why don't you take a little rest now while I finish washing the dishes?" and she stroked her mother's hair as the old woman obediently closed her eyes.

Slipping her fingers through the fine white strands, Maggie gazed with love and pity at her mother's face. With her eyes closed, her mother could be like any other old woman, just growing a bit more forgetful as years passed. Sometimes, Maggie could almost convince herself that this particular fantasy was real.

But then her mother would open her eyes to gaze blankly at her surroundings. The confusion that had been hidden behind those paper-thin lids would be painful to see, as Maggie watched her mother struggle to recall some recognizable pattern from the fading fabric of memory.

Suddenly, her mother moved her head, pulling it free from her daughter's caressing fingers.

"Leave me be," she said petulantly. "How can I sleep if you stand there bothering me?"

Maggie bit her lip, hurt by the sudden rejection.

"All right, Mama, I'll leave you alone. But call me if you need anything," and she slowly left her mother's side, returning to the kitchen where a pile of glasses and dishes waited to be washed and put away.

"Why did I decide to do this today?" she said aloud wearily, surveying the stack needing her attention. It was true the china cabinet was overdue for cleaning, but since her mother had come to stay, there was never enough time or energy for all those extra household chores.

Instead, there were endless trips to the grocery store, trying to keep abreast of her mother's strange and changeable food preferences; visits to the doctor and drug store, as medicines were tried, and, not surprisingly, failed to improve her mother's mental condition.

And there was finally the overwhelming and ever-present need to just keep track of her mother—to watch where she was, what she was doing. And to keep her own temper in check, especially on those days when her mother would follow her from room to room, asking the same questions over and over until Maggie wanted to scream with frustration.

She plunged the dishes into the sudsy water one by one, and as the dust was washed away, the colors glowed in the light. Maggie wished, not for the first time, there was something she could give her mother to wash away this cruel disease and bring back the living colors and shades of her memory.

"But there's nothing I can do," she whispered hopelessly, rinsing the dishes and setting them to drain.

There were no pills, no medicine, nothing to turn this forgetful old woman into the vibrant mother she once had been. All Maggie could do was stand by and watch her mother's mind weaken a little more each day, while her body, in an ironic twist, remained relatively strong—a prison for the dying mind.

It's like a deathwatch, she thought. And I can't even reach her to say good-bye.

"What are you doing?" Her mother's voice startled Maggie, lost in her thoughts.

"Are you awake already, Mama? I was just finishing up the last of the dishes from the china cupboard. Do you remember this set?" Maggie held up a bone china cup, rimmed with a delicate band of gold. "You used to tell me all about these when I was little. A wedding present to your grandmother. And these are the last two of the set."

The others had broken over the years. Old and delicate, too fragile to last through countless journeys through space and time.

And was that what happened to your mind, Mama? Maggie asked silently. Was it too fragile to take the strain of time as well?

Her mother glanced at the cup and then took it from Maggie's hand. "What a pretty pattern."

Maggie couldn't tell from her voice if she was remembering or just commenting on a design she hadn't seen before.

"Yes, it is lovely," Maggie agreed and then reached for the cup. "But I have to put it away now, Mama."

But even as she moved to take it, her mother clutched it tighter in her thin hand, now almost as fragile and translucent as the cup itself.

"I'd like a cup of tea, Maggie," she said firmly. "I'm very thirsty and a cup would be nice right now. I think I'll make it myself" and she moved toward the stove. "I'll just brew a pot and pour it into this cup."

"I'd rather we used another one, Mama," Maggie said, trying to infuse her words with all the persuasion she could muster. "That cup is old—hot tea might shatter it."

She offered her mother a plastic mug but the old woman shook her head.

"This cup, Maggie. I want this one. I never get to drink out of it any more. And it used to be mine, you know," she added sharply. "I don't know why you are making such an issue."

Maggie sighed. Her mother was going to be difficult about the cup, as she had been lately about so many things. It wasn't that her mother cared what she drank from, Maggie knew. It was more as if she was testing Maggie's patience, trying to see how far she could push her daughter before she got angry.

It's like dealing with a two-year-old in a seventy-five-year-old body, Maggie thought. There was no reasoning with her at times like this. There was nothing she could do, except wait until her mother's attention was captured by something else and

Maggie could retrieve the cup, now held so carelessly in that bony hand.

She glanced at the stove and realized her mother had switched on the wrong burner, which was now beginning to heat, perilously close to her mother's outstretched fingers.

"Mama!" Maggie reached forward to pull her mother's hand away from the glowing element a fraction of a second before the skin could be burned. But her mother, startled by the sudden motion, released her hold on the cup, and it shattered on the hardwood floor.

"I'm sorry, Maggie," her mother said worriedly, glancing up at her daughter, but Maggie shook her head.

"Let me see your hand, Mama," and she turned her toward the light, searching for blisters on the wrinkled skin. "Did you get hurt?"

"No, I'm fine. Really, Maggie. I didn't get hurt at all. I can't imagine how it happened," and she looked at the stove accusingly. "I'm sure I turned on the right burner. I didn't mean to break the cup," she added sadly, but Maggie only sighed, releasing her mother's hand.

"It doesn't matter, Mama," bending down to pick up the shattered fragments. "It was only a cup, after all. Why don't you sit down and I'll finish the tea."

"I don't think I want any after all, Maggie," her mother answered, sitting down at the small kitchen table. "You just go on with what you were doing and don't worry about me. I'll be fine," and she smiled anxiously at her daughter.

Maggie mustered a smile in response. It was almost as though her mother was afraid of her, afraid she'd roused her anger by breaking the cup.

But it was just an accident, Maggie told herself. Next time, I'll have to be more careful about letting Mama hold things.

And for a brief second, there flashed across her mind an endless succession of days spent keeping a closer and closer eye on her mother—watching her every move, trying to gauge her every thought—until the line blurred between mother and daughter and they merged into one.

"It doesn't matter," she repeated to herself and wasn't certain if she meant the cup or her ever-increasing responsibilities. It didn't matter. Maggie had to do it. This was her mother, after all.

"I'll just finish drying these dishes," she said aloud, "and then I'll start getting supper ready. Roast and potatoes and carrots, remember?" she added, before her mother could ask.

Her mother nodded her head. "Carrots in honey sauce," she said, surprising Maggie, who hadn't expected her to respond. "You said you'd do them like that for me. That's how I used to make them when you were little, Maggie. Lots of honey and butter," and she smiled, as though recalling a small child carefully spearing one golden ring after another, dripping with the sweet syrup.

Maggie held her breath. Her mother's lucid moments were rare and precious, for one never knew which one would be the last, which memory would be the final one snatched from the gathering mists.

But "I think I'd like a cup of tea now, Maggie," and the spell was broken, leaving Maggie to yearn for the other recollections of her childhood trapped inside her mother's mind.

She sighed. "I'll make it now, Mama. It will just take a moment," and the kitchen was silent, broken only by the sound of water heating in the kettle, and finally, the high thin sound of the whistle as the water reached the boiling point.

Maggie poured it into the waiting pot, and, as the tea steeped, dried the last few pieces of china. At least *that* job is done, she thought resignedly. It may have taken all day but now it can be crossed off the list.

The list itself seemed endless, with more items added than removed, especially in the last few weeks. Her mother's condition was a series of downward-turning spirals, with the deterioration increasing almost daily. It was almost as though her mother was gradually releasing her hold on reality, allowing her mind to drift farther away while Maggie watched helplessly from the shore, unable to bring her back.

"Here's your tea, Mama," and Maggie put the steaming cup on the table. "Watch, it's hot."

Her mother paused to blow gently on the surface before taking a careful sip. "It's good, Maggie."

Maggie relaxed and smiled.

"I'm glad, Mama," she answered warmly. "You finish it while I start supper. I'll get the carrots sliced," pulling them from the refrigerator, "and then you can tell me how to make the sauce."

She glanced at her mother as she set the scrubbed carrots in a pile on the table, hoping that the mention of the sauce would trigger another memory, another precious story of Maggie's childhood.

The older woman reached over to pull a carrot from the stack, and Maggie's heart leaped. She stopped slicing the golden spears and asked casually, "Do you want to help me, Mama?"

Her mother looked up at her. "Are these for dinner?"

"Yes, Mama." Maggie's smile began to fade but she determinedly kept her voice light. "I was going to clean them and then you would tell me how to make the sauce. With honey and butter. Remember?" She was unaware of the trace of desperation that had crept into her voice. "Like you used to make for me, Mama, when I was little."

Her mother frowned. "I don't like carrots, Maggie. I like potatoes and spinach and maybe even celery—I don't know, I can't remember…" Her forehead crinkled in thought before smoothing out again. "But I know I don't like carrots."

Maggie was still, the carrot slices a tarnished heap before her.

"No, I don't like carrots, never did," her mother stated firmly. "How about green beans instead, nice fresh ones? What are we having for dinner, Maggie?"

NANCY CHRISTIE

WHEN ANN CALLS

"What about 'Kate'? Kate, Katherine, Katie, Katerina..."

She tried the names out, savoring the sound of them, imagining herself calling them—"Katie, come get your snack!" "Katerina, it's time for your nap!"

"No, not 'Kate.'" The old man folded his newspaper, keeping one finger tucked firmly inside so he could find where he had left off reading. "It makes me think of Katherine Hepburn and you know how I feel about her."

"You don't like her because she was independent," the old woman retorted, but with little heat. It was an old familiar argument after all.

"I didn't like her because she didn't know her place," he answered with finality before returning to the obituary column. So rarely did they see any of their old acquaintances that he had come to rely on the newspaper for news of someone's passing.

"All right, not Kate, then. But how about Elizabeth? That's a nice old-fashioned name," but the old man didn't answer her. She didn't mind. Most evenings he didn't answer her, partly because with age had come a loss of hearing, partly because after fifty years, he had probably heard everything she had to say, and given every conceivable response. But still, he could show *some* interest.

She remembered what she was doing when Ann had called with the news: frying up some liver and onions for supper, and the smell of the onions had brought tears to her eyes.

Ann thought she was crying about the news. "Really, Mother," she had said, with the exasperated tone that so often colored her words, "I'm only having a child. There is no need to cry about anything."

Anyway, ever since Ann had let them know about her baby, she had been unable to think of anything else. Baby names, baby clothes, the smell of baby powder, and the feel of baby skin—Sarah delved deep into her own past and brought back those magical moments, from the time she knew she was expecting to the time when Ann was brought to her, "wrapped in swaddling clothes" like the Biblical story of Jesus' birth.

She had hoped to see more of Ann, had longed to watch her daughter grow heavy with child, but instead, months passed since the call and all she could do was imagine the fullness of her daughter's belly, the swelling of her breasts. Sometimes, she would place her hand on her own soft, flabby abdomen and try to recall the flutter of a baby's movement, how it seemed her insides were turning upside down as the baby kicked and turned and rolled.

So long ago—she was nearly forty-one when Ann was born, and now Ann herself was in her late thirties. She had named her daughter after her husband's mother, in an attempt to soften the old woman's attitude toward her son's wife. Instead, she had unwittingly imbued her daughter with her grandmother's personality. Cold, severe, distant—those adjectives could just as easily have been applied to the child as to the elder.

From the time she was old enough to express her own individuality, Ann had been stubbornly resistant to affectionate gestures and pet names.

"My name is 'Ann,'" she would insist, when Sarah made the mistake of calling her Annie or Anna or any one of a dozen endearments like "sweetheart." She was more forgiving of her father, perhaps because he so rarely spoke to her. But she resisted any show of affection from her mother, leaving the old woman to hold it all inside.

Her husband finished reading the paper, the signal that it was time to shut off the lights and go to bed. For more years than she could count, they had followed the same routine, but tonight, she was reluctant to put away the book of baby names.

"I might stay up a bit longer," she said, half-hoping he would stay with her, read through the book, and find a name that he liked. "Besides, Ann might call. Did you check the machine when we came back from the grocer's?"

It was a new answering machine, bought at Sarah's insistence. Although they spent most of each day in the house, she wanted to be absolutely sure that if Ann called while they were out, they would know it. Each time they returned home, she eagerly scanned the face of the small black box, hoping that the red light would be pulsing, signaling a call from their child. Each time, she was disappointed.

"I checked it. You checked it. There was no call," he said impatiently, then softened his tone when he saw her face, so transparent in its pain. "Ann is busy, Sarah. She works long hours. We'll hear from her, I'm sure."

"But you think she would have called by now. You think she would answer me, tell me what names she liked, or if there was another name she had decided upon..." Her voice broke as she thought of the messages she had left for her daughter: *Ann, this is your mother. What do you think of Susan for a name? Or maybe Megan? Ann, how are you feeling? Is the baby kicking yet?*

She couldn't understand why Ann never returned the phone calls. She couldn't be *that* busy. Or could it be that something was wrong, that the pregnancy was in danger and she didn't want to worry her parents...

"That's it," she told her husband, still standing there, waiting for her to rise from her chair. "There is something wrong and she won't tell me. She doesn't want me to worry. But if she would call, I could comfort her. I could tell her that it will be all right. I could pray for her at church on Sunday. If she would only call..."

"There is nothing wrong," he said. "Ann is busy. Besides, you know she doesn't call us often. She *never* did. Why would you expect things to be different now?"

Because they *are* different, she said to herself, as she rose with difficulty from her seat. Her knees ached more in this cold, damp weather. She wondered if she would be able to push the baby's stroller in the spring or if the ache would be too much to bear. At least she would be able to rock the child, hold the small body close to her heart and feel its own heartbeat, an echo of hers but stronger, faster.

Ann would surely come to visit once the baby was born, she thought, changing into her cotton nightgown and running a brush through her short white hair. She would at least want her parents to see their only grandchild.

"Wouldn't she?" she asked, turning to her husband, but he had drawn the covers up over his shoulders and was already gently snoring.

Of course, her daughter would come, she decided, turning back to the mirror. She set the brush down. Perhaps Ann didn't want her to suggest baby names. Perhaps Ann thought she was interfering. Pregnant women get such strange ideas.

I won't call her with any more names, she decided. After all, naming a baby is something the mother should do on her own. Instead, I'll make a quilt for the baby's crib. What color should I choose: yellow or green, pink or blue? Or maybe a patchwork quilt in case the baby is a boy—although Sarah was certain it would be a girl, a delicate, blue-eyed, golden-haired child.

I'll call Ann tomorrow and ask her if she had chosen the colors for the baby's room, she thought as she climbed into bed to lie next to her husband. I won't tell her about the quilt, though. I want it to be a surprise.

She tried to picture Ann's face when she opened the box holding the soft colorful comforter. But the image wouldn't come. So Sarah focused instead on the quilt itself: the fine, straight stitches that bordered the blocks of color, the satin ribbon trimming the edges.

I'll choose the pattern tomorrow, she thought to herself sleepily. And when Ann calls, she can tell me what colors to use. But I won't buy the material until I hear from her. I'll wait until then—when Ann calls.

PERIPHERAL VISIONS AND OTHER STORIES

THE ACCIDENT

When the telephone rang for the fourth time in a row, Margaret frowned in impatience. She had so looked forward to an afternoon of quiet while Megan played at Billy's house, but the interruptions usually caused by one small five-year-old had been replaced by those of the telephone.

The insistent ringing continued as she slid one of the filled cookie sheets from the oven, heat flushing her pale face. It didn't stop until Margaret lifted the receiver and wedged it against her cheek, all the while struggling to remove the chocolate chip cookies—Megan's favorite—from the pan.

"Hello," she said impatiently, as one cookie crumbled beneath the rough thrust of the spatula. "Yes, this is Margaret Adams."

The voice on the other end spoke briefly, but it was enough to still her busy hands.

She answered, "Yes, right away," and carefully set the phone back down. It wasn't until the smell of burning chocolate invaded the kitchen that Margaret began again to move—slowly, stiffly, as though a painful eternity had passed since the telephone call.

She didn't cry, not when she slipped on her jacket and found Megan's mittens still in her left pocket. Nor when she had to wheel Megan's tricycle out from behind the car—how many times had she told her daughter to park it alongside the wall?

And she still didn't cry, not even when the harried doctor in the busy emergency room used words like "unfortunate" and "unavoidable."

"The police think he couldn't stop in time," he said, leaning tiredly against the wall. There were so many victims yet to see. Weekends were always full of accidents.

Margaret's hands crumpled the red mittens into a ball, and then smoothed them out again. Not enough time? she thought. Not even for my daughter?

"It wasn't his fault," he continued, as though it made a difference.

Margaret nodded but wondered whose fault it had been: Megan's, because she didn't stop to look before running out in the street? Or was it Margaret's fault after all—for allowing Megan to play at someone else's house, for not warning her enough about traffic hazards, for being safe at home baking cookies while her daughter died.

"I should have made her wear her mittens," holding them out for the doctor to see. "Her skin gets so chapped,"

He frowned briefly, thinking to himself that she shouldn't be alone, that shock does strange things to people. Perhaps some medication…

"I'll take you to her."

But she continued, as though he hadn't spoken at all. "I bought them because they matched her coat. She looked so pretty all dressed in red."

"This way," and not ungently, he took her arm, leading her to the cubicle where Megan lay.

She looked like she was sleeping, Margaret thought in surprise. Except for the bruised side of her face and the lack of color in her cheeks, she might be sleeping. Even now, if Margaret just shook her a bit, Megan might awaken, might open her eyes and...

"Nurse," the doctor said softly, indicating with a nod of his head Margaret's presence. And then he was gone.

"She needs a haircut," Margaret said to the white-uniformed woman. "I wanted to take her this afternoon but she wanted to play at Billy's house." And was that why it happened? she asked herself. Because I looked forward to an afternoon of quiet?

"So we settled on tomorrow for the hair," stroking back the too-long curls from the pale forehead, "and instead I baked her favorite cookies."

I was also going to read that new book from the library, she remembered. When Megan's home, she interrupts me so often I can never read a story straight through.

The nurse reached out to touch Margaret's arm, but she rejected the gesture of sympathy, continuing in the same toneless voice.

"I wonder where Billy's mother is," all the while still running her fingers through the pale golden strands. "I would think she'd be here to tell me what happened."

She leaned forward to gently straighten the sheet over the narrow shoulders.

"She's waiting in the hall," the nurse answered, knowing all the while that it would be better if the mother cried, screamed, anything to let the feeling escape.

"Thank you," Margaret said, and with one last look, she slipped past the nurse in search of the woman who was to have watched over Megan.

It was easy to pick out Billy's mother from the crowd of people in the waiting room. She was standing off to the side, one hand holding a sodden tissue, the other keeping a protective grasp on her frightened son.

"Margaret," she said, catching sight of her," I don't know what to tell you. One minute they were playing in the yard and the next thing I knew Billy was screaming that a truck had hit Megan and she wasn't moving."

She started crying again but Margaret stood there, dry-eyed.

"I'm so sorry, I'm so sorry...," drifting helplessly to a close.

Margaret ignored her, and knelt down in front of the little boy.

"Tell me what happened," she said, and the child swallowed hard before answering.

"We were playing ball and I guess I threw it too hard. It went over her head. But I didn't mean for her to get hurt—honest," and his voice quavered as he tried to hold back the tears. "I just wanted to play."

Why were they playing in the front yard? Margaret asked silently. Why did he have to throw the ball so hard?

She rose to her feet, still looking at the young child with her clear cold gaze. Then she said, "I wish you had gotten that damn ball instead of my daughter," before turning away, not caring that Billy's mother stared at her in horror or that the boy had started to cry.

Crying wouldn't help, she knew, and her eyes remained dry as she signed papers and made arrangements at the desk. There were procedures for everything in this world, even death. It was pointless to cry, because it wouldn't bring Megan back. Tears wouldn't wash away the inescapable feeling that if she had done something differently, Megan would still be with her.

Once home, she wandered through the rooms, not sure what she should do, what she should think, how she should react.

"I should have spent more time with her," picking up the dog-eared book of bedtime stories she sometimes read to Megan. But there were other nights—too many?—when she had refused to read because she was tired from working all day.

"I should have done more with her," recalling the promises she would make to Megan: next week, they would go to the movies, next month, the zoo. She never thought the limitless tomorrows would come to such a final, terrible end.

She found herself in Megan's room. "Everything is so dusty," she said, noticing how the furniture's warm glow was obscured by a slight film. She was going to clean Megan's room after baking, she remembered. Then, when Megan would come home, they would eat cookies and read stories...

Margaret collected the cleaning cloths and began polishing the furniture, wiping away the countless smudges and fingerprints from the smooth surface, all the signs that proved Megan had once been there.

Then, she cleaned the window, blurred where Megan liked to rest her forehead as she watched the robins building a nest in the tree. Ruthlessly, Margaret scrubbed away all traces of her daughter from the glass, leaving it shining and mirror-bright.

In its reflection, she saw a woman with pale skin and empty eyes, and for a moment, wondered who it could be. It couldn't be Megan's mother. She no longer existed, just as there was nothing left of the child who had once been Margaret's daughter.

"If I'd been a better mother this wouldn't have happened. It's my fault," she said aloud, and it was easier to believe in a vengeful God, far easier than to think there was no reason at all for Megan's death.

Megan... it had only been that morning since her daughter had kissed her good-bye, but now Margaret stood still, unable to remember the feel of Megan's arms around her neck, the scent of her hair after it had been washed, the way her voice sounded. It was all part of her punishment. She would never be able to recall her daughter clearly.

She turned away from the window, and went over to the shelf where Megan had arranged all her stuffed toys. One by one, she picked them up, smoothed the clothes, the hair, and then set each in its place, just the way Megan did every evening. She tried to picture her daughter, but couldn't—couldn't quite make out her hands touching the toys with such tenderness, couldn't quite hear the small voice whispering secrets to her silent companions.

The room was clean now. Past five—had it all happened today? Too much sadness for just a few hours. Too much for a day or week or month. Too much, even, for a lifetime—and the streetlights came on, lighting the darkness outside. Margaret gave the room one final look and then realized Roger was missing: Roger, the stuffed bear Megan always slept with.

She had to find the bear. Megan wouldn't sleep without the bear in her arms.

She went from room to room, absentmindedly picking up Megan's belongings from where she had left them scattered throughout the house.

"Maybe he's in one of the closets," she said aloud, rummaging through the dark corners and high shelves in vain. The garage? But a thorough search yielded nothing that resembled Roger, with his button eyes and black paws and silly grin, slightly worn from all of Megan's kisses.

Two hours later, Margaret stood in the kitchen, looking around her as though she expected the toy to materialize.

"Where is that damned bear?" she cried in frustration, her voice echoing in the silence. "Why can't I find him?" and she slammed her fist against the wall with such force that the picture of Megan hanging nearby trembled on its hook.

She pulled open drawers, slamming them shut again.

"Where is he?" The anger built up as the bear continued to elude her. "What did she do with him? Why couldn't she be more careful with her belongings?"

The cabinet doors squealed on their hinges as she continued her search.

"She was supposed to take care of him! He was her bear, after all!" and her voice grew louder. "Why couldn't she be more careful!" and the last door was shut so hard it flew open again, narrowly missing Margaret's head.

As suddenly as it came, the anger drained from Margaret and she sank to the floor, resting her throbbing head against the refrigerator.

"Why couldn't she be more careful?" she whispered and it wasn't the bear she was thinking of but the ball and the truck and, finally, Megan, lying still and silent and so far away.

She might have stayed there for hours, staring blindly at nothing, but the doorbell rang, piercing the silence of the house. And when she opened the door, it took her a moment to realize it was Billy, small and frightened, on her doorstep.

"She left him at my house," and Margaret saw he was holding Roger tenderly in his arms, the way a mother might cradle a newborn. The way she had once held Megan when she was tiny and fresh and all her own. "But he's lonely, so I brought him home. He misses her, I think." And gently, Billy's small hand stroked the bear.

Margaret was silent, watching as he gave the bear one final pat and then held it out to her. "I'm sorry about Megan," he whispered and then turned and ran from the silent woman, leaving behind the bear clutched in her cold hands.

Margaret closed the door behind him, all the while still holding the bear. Then she buried her face in his fur, inhaling the faint scent that was Megan.

And now, with eyes tightly shut, she could see Megan again: pictures of Megan as they went for walks and put puzzles together and cuddled at night while Margaret read fairy tales.

Pictures of Megan: eyes shining and smile gap-toothed and endearing, when Margaret would pick her up at the sitter's each night.

And almost, she could feel Megan's arms around her. Almost she could hear her daughter say she loved her.

"I tried to be good," she whispered into the soft fur of the bear. "Why did it have to happen?" And in asking, she realized there would never be an answer, that Megan's death wasn't anyone's fault, and couldn't be laid at anyone's door.

PERIPHERAL VISIONS AND OTHER STORIES

She pulled the stuffed bear closer, and the scent of Megan grew stronger in her memory as she began at last to cry.

NANCY CHRISTIE

'TIL DEATH DO US PART

"It's a gift for you, darling," said Richard, smiling winningly at his wife, whom he had vowed to kill as soon as the ink on the insurance policy had dried. "I chose it especially for you."

Elizabeth eyed the package with suspicion, rather than appreciation. The last few gifts she had received from Richard had not only been notable failures, but downright dangerous as well.

There was the electric carving knife, for example: a gift for her first birthday as a married woman. It had unaccountably released both shining blades the moment Elizabeth laid it against the crisp skin of the Thanksgiving turkey. Fortunately, she had very quick reflexes, which enabled her to dodge the flying metal strips as they came with deadly aim toward her slender throat.

Then there was the bright red ten-speed bike: an intriguing mix of glittering gears and sinuous cables. Unfortunately, one of the cables was not attached to the brakes, a fact Elizabeth discovered on the downhill run of a particularly steep hill.

Leaping off to land in a knee-skinning bit of gravel, Elizabeth saw her bike miss the turn, sail into the ocean, and sink into watery obscurity—all while Richard stood watching in disbelief at the top of the hill.

And, once again, as he had been when the knife malfunctioned, Richard was apologetic, remorseful, and deeply distressed.

He was also deeply disappointed, Elizabeth knew. To have put so much effort into a goal, and then be forced to watch it all go up in smoke—which was exactly what happened to the curling iron she received for her next birthday. Seconds after Elizabeth wound some strands of her silvery blonde hair around it, it began to smoke. And spit. And spark.

It singed the ends of her carefully-cut coiffure—ruining for weeks her hairdresser's best efforts—and very nearly singed Elizabeth's scalp as well.

Fortunately, and with utter disregard for the future of her hairdo, Elizabeth yanked the sparking iron from her head, just as Richard came around the corner to view the performance of his latest gift.

Elizabeth would have been quite upset over these "accidents" had she not been responsible for a few of her own. Not having Richard's ability for mechanical alteration, she settled on choosing one subject and finding out all she could about its operations. By the time she finished every book she could get on electrical energy, Elizabeth would have been quite adept at re-wiring an outlet or installing a light fixture. However, this was not her intention.

Her first foray into homicide was a bit amateurish, she had to admit. The electric shaver did in fact short-circuit, but the resulting shock was about par with inserting a key into an outlet: slightly painful, but hardly deadly. Richard's expression immediately following the incident was a blend of shock and dismay—the latter, she surmised, because he had hoped for something a little more creative for her first attempt.

Not wanting to disappoint him, she sought to prove herself worthy with her next gift. And, in retrospect, the electric blanket operation was one of which she was justly proud. It had taken her a week of practice to learn exactly how much insulation must be removed before the bare wires would set the acrylic fibers on fire. Then, with Machiavellian cunning, she hid the blanket under her stack of sweaters in the closet until Richard's next birthday, when she could present him with a gift worthy of her talents.

Fortunately, a cold spell coincided with the happy day, and as she gave him the package, she remarked that it was certain to put an end to his frozen-feet syndrome. How permanently she could only hope, she thought as she departed for her own room far down the hallway from his.

And the fire was everything a pyromaniac could hope for: snapping and crackling merrily along the mattress, with a little cloud of smoke puffing from beneath carefully tucked-in corners. Unfortunately, Richard wasn't present when it started, having left the room to raid the refrigerator for a late-night snack. But when he returned, he found the bed a great deal warmer but certainly less hospitable than when he left it.

His expression that night definitely held more admiration for his clever wife.

But her *pièce de résistance* was undoubtedly the whirlpool machine, a gift for Richard's last birthday. Elizabeth had carefully unboxed the bulky contraption and set it in the gleaming porcelain tub—after a few small but important adjustments.

Then she waited for Richard to enjoy what would be for him a new, and hopefully last, experience.

It was only by an incredible stroke of luck—good for Richard but not so good for Fluffy, their French poodle—that the small dog decided to race its master for the joys of the bath.

In a flash, Fluffy became a French hot dog. And Elizabeth was left waiting for *her* birthday and another "unique" gift from Richard.

Once more, Elizabeth looked at the small package, gaily decorated with ribbons and bows. And while she was considering how such a small box could possibly be a threat to her continued existence, Richard watched her closely, wondering if this would be, quite literally, the gift to end all gifts—and gift-giving.

He had to admit that he had enjoyed the challenge. Certainly nothing during their brief courtship had indicated Elizabeth to be anything more than a well-bred and remarkably wealthy young woman with a great many decades ahead of her—years Richard was determined to reduce as quickly as possible. But the past three had revealed hidden depths to his wife's character.

He had been wise enough, he congratulated himself, to wait nearly a year before putting his plans in motion. Unfortunately, he had not counted on failure, nor on Elizabeth catching on quite as quickly as she had. Before too long, the couple found themselves taking turns playing the roles of murderer and victim—with neither being able to kill or be killed.

That had been a frustrating turn of events, Richard acknowledged as he ran his hand through his slightly thinning hair, and one that Elizabeth had taken with better grace and patience than he had.

He had rushed a bit on that last one, he realized now. The curling iron probably wouldn't have set her afire even if she hadn't noticed the sparks and sizzles. Now the electric blanket—he had to give Elizabeth full marks for that one. The time and effort she had expended, not to mention all the careful planning, was really amazing. For a moment, as he had stood there watching his favorite robe go up in flames (along with the mattress, box springs, and pillows), he felt a strong sense of approbation for the woman he had married. And he vowed to do his best to maintain the level of cleverness they had jointly achieved.

Elizabeth slowly unwrapped the slim package to find inside a slender brown wallet filled with traveler's checks and two tickets for a week-long cruise to some little-known Pacific islands, and was overcome, both with surprise and dismay. It was so unlike Richard to have spent so much money to achieve his goal, and to do it in such a (she mentally shook her head over the adjective) splashy fashion!

She glanced at him in wonder. The man had hidden depths, probably as deep as the waters they would be sailing on. She vowed to never underestimate him again as long as she lived. Which, if she had anything to do with it, would be at least as long as he did.

But first there was the cruise, and Elizabeth's dismay grew. Richard must really be desperate, for the only thing the two of them had in common was a dislike of being in the water. In Elizabeth's case, that even extended to swimming pools, for of all the sports she had tried, swimming was the only one at which she was a notable failure. A bathtub was the closest she wished to be to total immersion. And there was nothing she hated more than the thought of an ocean cruise, surrounded as she would be by all that insubstantial liquid. But she was a sporting girl and had to give Richard his turn at bat, however unpleasant the circumstances.

After all, she thought, turning the tickets over in her hand, Richard was making some sacrifices as well. He was a terrible sailor, she knew, turning green at the gills as soon as water became anything less than a smooth mirrored surface. He had to be given full credit for his courage in using such a method to achieve his goal.

Elizabeth made up her mind. Such courage should be rewarded.

Crossing to where Richard sat in an agony of expectation, she gave him a resounding kiss and bone-crushing hug.

"Darling, it's wonderful!" she exclaimed. "It's exactly what we both need—a change of scenery to stimulate our imagination!"

Richard paused in his moment of self-congratulation. There was something about her tone, something that made him wonder if he would be able to accomplish his aim. He hadn't expected her to see through him quite so quickly, although by now it was no secret what they were both up to.

But he had purposely made the arrangements to give her the least amount of time for preparation. The scheme was bound to work—had to, in fact, because he had dropped quite a bundle on the trip. But he rose to the challenge, refusing to let Elizabeth see his moment of unease.

"Yes, the trip will be wonderful," he agreed. "Just the two of us alone, watching the dolphins at play."

And the sharks at supper, thought Elizabeth, but smiled at Richard anyway. He deserved her full attention as a reward for all the money he had spent.

"But what about the waves, Richard?" she asked, wondering if in the heat of creativity he had forgotten his own weakness.

Richard moved a bit in his chair, and then gave her a weak smile.

"Well, I suppose there will be a bit of roughness, but not too much," he said, his stomach churning in advance. "But it's only until we round the last island and then it will be smooth. The captain promised," he added, with an emphasis on the words to reassure his treacherous digestive system. "And the best part of the cruise," he added, resolutely turning his mind from the vision of waves sweeping over the deck to carry him off, "is all the time we will spend alone—watching the stars from the topmost deck, dancing alone under a full moon. I just can't wait!" and the arm he had thrown carelessly around his wife tightened in anticipation.

"But surely we won't be the only ones on the cruise," she said.

"Not exactly, my love," he answered, with a smile. "There's a group of retired people on board as well. But they will probably be spending all their time playing shuffleboard or bingo. We'll be able to explore the ship and enjoy late night strolls, all by ourselves."

"How romantic," Elizabeth breathed, but her mind thought of more appropriate adjectives. Alone? On deck? With Richard at her side? His hands at her throat? His strong arms lifting her over the edge? She could see it now: an innocent embrace, a stumble, and there goes Elizabeth into the icy depths. She shivered as the cold seawater of her imaginings closed over her head and privately resolved to steer clear of any deserted portions of the ship when her spouse was at her side.

She didn't swim and didn't have time to learn—not in the two days before they set sail. She doubted if she could even master the Dead Man's Float in forty-eight hours, although with Richard's assistance she was sure to be an expert at it by cruise end.

This was undoubtedly the best of all the gifts, and try as she might, Elizabeth couldn't see a way of escaping her watery fate. Not without outside assistance, anyway, but that wouldn't be sporting. After all, Richard never once mentioned the lack of insulation to the firefighters. She was honor-bound to meet and defeat this challenge on her own.

Watching his wife's brow furrow in concentration, Richard was well pleased with the results of his gift. Despite the discomfort he was bound to endure, he was certain the outcome would make it all worthwhile. This time of year, cruises weren't heavily booked, and it would be practically impossible for Elizabeth to avoid being alone with him at some part of the day or night. All it would take was one quick push... and unconsciously, Richard's shoulders tensed in anticipation.

But a bit of regret colored his joy. These past three years with Elizabeth had certainly been exciting, and although he planned to marry as soon as it was decently possible (to another wealthy woman, of course), he knew that no other female could match Elizabeth for inventiveness. The years ahead seemed doomed to boredom, and for a fleeting moment, he regretted the economic necessity that forced him to continue along this path. For the first time, Richard wondered if the money would make up for all the excitement that would drown along with Elizabeth.

#

The day of the cruise dawned clear and sunny, but with the thought of all those cresting waves, Richard was unable to concentrate on his packing. He fidgeted about so much that Elizabeth finally had to finish the job, looking at him curiously all the while. Could he be regretting his plan?

Her own emotions were a bit mixed. She had found marriage to Richard to be exciting and challenging, adjectives she would never have applied to her parents' forty-year union. And looking back, she couldn't help wondering what life would have been like if she had obeyed her first instinct and not wed the personable man who had come calling. It would have been safer, she knew, but certainly quite dull.

And if he hadn't started this ridiculous campaign to go from husband to widower in the shortest time possible, she would have probably been quite content to sew curtains and grow flowers...

Flowers—now there was an idea! Didn't deadly nightshade come from flowers? Elizabeth shook her head and concentrated on the packing. This was Richard's turn. No fair planning ahead.

Richard stood by the window, watching for the taxi and smoking his seventh cigarette of the morning—a sure sign of worry. Finally, he turned to his wife and burst out, "It's the water, you know! I'm nervous about the waves and all that!"

Elizabeth's face cleared. Of course, Richard was simply afraid of seasickness. She smiled.

"Didn't I tell you?" she asked casually, holding up a small bottle of liquid. "I stopped at the drug store and got you some medicine for nausea. The druggist said it was just the thing for cramps."

Just the thing to cause them, Elizabeth thought privately as she slipped the bottle of ipecac into his shaving kit. One spoonful, and everything that had gone down would come back up. Quite violently, as a matter of fact. Between the medicine and the waves, Richard was bound to spend most of his time writhing in agony in his bunk, which ought to keep Elizabeth safe and dry. And since the drug wasn't fatal, she wasn't violating their unspoken code of ethics.

Richard eyed her suspiciously, and then decided that the medicine was probably what she had claimed it to be. After all, aside from her annual attempts on his life, she had always looked after him. He smiled gratefully, and then, as the taxi rounded the corner, carried the luggage downstairs.

It took some time for everyone to board, and both Richard and Elizabeth were in an agony of impatience until the ship finally set sail. With all the other passengers, they crowded to the deck and tossed bits of confetti toward the rapidly retreating shoreline. The atmosphere was festive, and in the excitement, Richard slipped an arm around his wife's shoulder, squeezing it so tightly she thought it would be dislocated.

"Happy, darling?" he asked, while she fought for breath.

"Ecstatic, sweetheart," she finally responded, and reaching an arm around his waist, she punched him just where she thought his kidneys might be. "You're such a wonderful husband," she added, noting his tears of pain with satisfaction. Her knowledge of human physiology was limited but accurate. "I just know I'm going to love this cruise!"

Behind them, two elderly ladies with smiles on their faces were watching the romantic antics of the couple.

"Isn't it wonderful?" whispered one to the other. "And they say romance in marriage is dead!"

LITTLE BOY FOUND

"I'll have coffee—but only if it's freshly brewed," she said firmly to the waitress. "And for Jerry, hot chocolate, but no whipped cream. Jerry's my grandson," she added, and he didn't contradict her.

The first time she had said that, she explained to him later that they were playing a game, "a 'Let's Pretend' game, like actors in a movie. We're pretending that I'm your grandma and you're my grandson Jerry. It'll be fun. You'll see!" And she had smiled at him, and he smiled back, uncertain but willing to please.

And it *was* fun at first. She would let him order anything he wanted: hamburgers for breakfast and ice cream sundaes for supper. And if it was hard to get comfortable in the car, eventually he figured out how to curl up with the seatbelt wrapped tightly around his waist so, even if she rounded a curve too fast, he didn't slide onto the floor.

But gradually, it had changed. *She* had changed. Now they only had two meals a day, or on bad days (not that he knew what made it a bad day, just that it *was* one), only one. He learned not to complain, not to ask questions, not to do or say anything that would bring on *that* look—eyes dead staring, lips as straight and merciless as the desert highway—the look that didn't go away until she released the fury building up inside her.

The first time, just a few hours after it all started, he tugged at her arm (how big she had seemed to him then! He barely reached her waist!) and asked, "When am I going home?

You said you were taking me there. I want to see my mommy," and he started to cry.

He was scared, even more scared than when he looked around the crowded aisles and realized that his mother was nowhere to be seen. So many people, but then, it was December and everyone was doing their holiday shopping.

"But not for toys," his mother had said, smiling. "Santa brings toys! But let's get some new ornaments for the tree. And maybe a different treetop—what about a star this year instead of the angel?"

And he had agreed, not really caring what they put on the tree as long as what he wanted would be there waiting for him on Christmas Day.

And that's when it happened—when his mother went down the aisle to get the treetop and she had to let go of his hand because she needed to reach for the one on the high shelf that she wanted and he knew he was supposed to stay right there, right by her. But there were so many people and everyone was trying to get what *they* wanted and no one cared about a little boy who couldn't see his mother anymore.

And so he went around the other side of the aisle, but she wasn't there either and then....

"You look lost, sweetie," the woman had said. "Do you want me to help you find your mommy?"

And he had agreed and she took his hand and he didn't even mind that she held it just a little too tightly because all he could think about was that someone was going to help him.

And then they were in a car and she was driving not too fast but fast enough so that pretty soon he couldn't tell where they were. All he knew was that it was taking too long and they were going too far. And that's when he asked, "When am I going home? You said you were taking me there. I want to see my mommy!" and she reached over and slapped him hard—just once, but once was enough—and all the while she kept driving.

He learned then that, in the end, it was better, safer, less painful to stay silent.

"Nothing to eat? We have fresh-baked pies," the waitress said, her pen poised above the pad. "Or maybe your grandson—Jerry, right?—would like some chocolate chip cookies." She smiled at him and he started to smile back, but then caught himself and looked down at his hands instead.

"No, thank you," and even though the words sounded friendly, he knew that she was beginning to get angry inside, a slow simmer that could easily boil over and submerge what self-control she had and result in a scalding—for him, not her.

He glanced up, trying to gauge just how angry she was, just how worried he had to be, and if there was something he could do to cool her down.

"Just the coffee and hot chocolate, *if* it isn't too much trouble," and he could tell that the waitress caught the warning underneath the apparently friendly words.

"Certainly, ma'am," and she looked at him again, still smiling, but he kept his lips straight and his eyes blank. She shrugged then and walked away to put in their order.

"Good boy, Jerry," the old woman said then. "Just like I always tell you: children should be seen and not heard."

The diner that night was busy and while they waited, he tried to pull the sleeves of his jacket down over his chapped wrists, but they were too short. The jacket had fit at first—

"Almost as though it had been bought just for you!" she had said gaily when she pulled it out of the trunk with the air of a magician pulling a rabbit from a hat. But that was six months ago and he had grown since then. Now whenever they would leave the car, the winter wind raked across the exposed areas, even though he shoved his fists as far as they could go into the too-small pockets.

"Here are your drinks," and the waitress set both mugs down on the table. But before she could turn away, the old woman thrust the coffee cup back at her.

"It's bitter. I said I wanted fresh-brewed."

He closed his eyes, hoping that when he opened them it would be all right, but there it was: the look. And even though it was directed at the waitress, he knew that it would be a bad night for him.

The waitress took the cup away and he hurriedly sipped his hot chocolate, even though he hated the too sweet, too hot drink. He never liked hot chocolate. His mother used to make him—what was it now? His brow crinkled with effort as he tried to remember. O, O —Ovaltine, that was it! The malted one, not the chocolate one. And she would pour it into his Mickey Mouse mug and then blow on it until it was just the right temperature.

He almost smiled but then stopped himself. She would ask why he was smiling and he didn't want to lie—couldn't lie, really, because she would *know* he was lying and that would be as bad as telling the truth. So instead he took a big gulp, the liquid burning his throat and bringing tears to his eyes. *That* was the reason for them, he told himself.

"That's better," the old woman said as she drank from the new cup the waitress had brought her. At least, *she* thought it was a new cup, but he suspected that it was the same one after all. He had caught the conspiratorial glance the young woman had sent to the other girl behind the counter and the grin she received in reply.

"Hurry up now, Jerry," and he drained his cup. They never stayed long in roadside diners, just long enough to get something to drink and use the bathroom. If it was time for a real meal, they took it to go—"Like having a picnic," she had said at first although now she gave no explanation. Or maybe she thought he didn't need one.

The woman dug a few bills out of her pocket and left them on the table along with the check, saying, "Come on, Jerry, we have to get going."

She used to tell him that they would come back in and tell the people at the counter that they were playing a game and that his real name was—what was it now? It had been so long since he had heard it, since he had told anyone what it was, that even he wasn't sure—but somehow that never happened. Instead they would leave the parking lot and head onto the highway, and then she would say it was too tricky to turn around with all the traffic. Or she would explain that they would come back the next morning, except that by the time the sun came up, they were in another town in another state and she said it would take too long to go back.

Now she didn't say anything anymore, which was just as well because he knew it would be a lie and he suspected that she knew that *he* knew that, and *that* would just make it worse.

They were almost at the car when the waitress came out after them.

"Young man? Jerry?" and he almost didn't turn around, almost didn't realize she was calling him, talking to him. "You left your hat!" And she waved the faded, stretched knit cap like a flag, the winter wind whipping her apron around her.

"Go get it," she hissed at him and he half ran back to take it, knowing that she was angry with him for drawing attention to them, for letting the waitress see the car they were in, for doing something—anything!—that was not planned.

The waitress pulled him a bit closer and tugged the hat over his head until it nearly covered his eyes. "There. Well, it's a little small but it's better than nothing. It's cold outside," the concern in her voice reminding him of his mother. "And here, this is for you," and she slipped something into his pocket. "It's a cookie. All little boys like cookies. You stay warm now, Jerry," and she gave him a quick squeeze.

For a moment he couldn't move. But then he heard the car horn and knew he had to go, right then, right now.

"Thank you," he said awkwardly, then headed back to where the headlights glittered like twin cat's eyes in the dark.

He was almost there but then something stopped him. Was it the cookie? The hug? The memory of someone else who once worried about him and maybe still did?

He looked back. The waitress was still waiting there, watching him. Squaring his shoulders, he took a deep breath, then, not caring what would happen, what *could* happen, he exhaled the words entwined in a lifeline of hope: "Paul! My name is Paul!"

I REMEMBER....

It was nearly two o'clock. Surely they would be coming any minute now, the old woman thought. Not that she was excited. It would be ridiculous to be excited about celebrating her birthday. After all, she'd had eighty-seven of them already. What could be different about this one?

Eighty-eight—how did she come to be so old? It was hard to believe that so much time had passed. There were times when she would look in a mirror to smooth her white hair into a more presentable bun and be startled and almost frightened to see the face of an old woman looking back at her. Where was that young woman? It was as though she had disappeared, and this old, arthritic body had come to take her place.

There was no one left who remembered her, no one who shared all the memories of a lifetime. They were all gone. During those long hours of night, when sleep eluded her, she would try to recall the way it had once been. But it seemed the memories had died as well, and she was left, watching the hands of the clock go around, and wondering if she had ever lived, or loved, at all.

But here (and she gave herself a mental shake), there was no point in thinking about what had been. Not today, anyway. It would be nice to see her grandson and his wife and daughter. They made the three-hour trip to see her every few weeks and always brought some kind of little gift for her—not that she needed anything.

Of course, it was Melanie who chose the present. Her granddaughter-in-law always picked what she thought were useful items: new slippers, a flannel nightgown or, for her last birthday, a heavy quilted robe. Melanie didn't know that most of the clothing she had given over the years was still waiting in her closet, the tags not even removed. The old woman was happy wearing the same clothing she had had for years, even her chenille cover-up, although it was patchworked with mended spots.

She'd had that robe for years—bought it before her husband had died. It had been good enough then. It was good enough now. It would be frivolous to cast it aside for something new. But then, that was something the younger people didn't understand.

"Where could they be?" she said aloud, crossing the small living room to pull aside the net curtain over the front window. They were usually here by one. Impatiently, she let the curtain fall back into place, and reached over to move the small picture from the end table to the mantelpiece. Young Jennifer was so full of energy after the trip, more energy than the small room could hold. It would be better if the picture was out of the way.

She paused for a moment, holding the silver frame tightly in her hand. It was her wedding picture, blurred and yellowed, with the two of them in stiff, unnatural poses. But they had counted themselves lucky to have a picture at all. If the man with a box camera hadn't been traveling through their village, there would have been no photograph at all to mark the occasion, and nothing for her to stare at for two long years, until she was able to join her husband.

"You're beautiful." His voice was soft with wonderment, and the slight tremor made her weaken inside. She had never been alone in a bedroom with a man before, and even though they were married and it was right and proper, she was still

afraid. Yet there was an undercurrent of anticipation, making her icy cold and unbearably hot all at once.

He had reached up and slowly pulled out the bone hairpins that secured her dark brown hair in a knot on top of her head, creating a veil between them and the outside world. And their kiss smelled of the lemons she had rubbed through her hair to make it shine.

The sound of a car pulling up out front brought her back to the present. Two doors slammed shut and then running feet—that would be young Jennifer, excited, impetuous, certain to fall and skin her knee before the afternoon was over.

"You ought to make her slow down," the old woman said as she opened the screen door to the mother and child, both with long blonde hair gleaming in the sunlight.

"Hi, Grandma," said Melanie, and then was pushed aside by Jennifer, who stood on tiptoe to kiss the old woman's cheek before rushing into the house, calling "Happy birthday, Grandma!" over her shoulder.

The old woman looked in vain for her grandson, before turning to the young woman still waiting on the doorstep.

"Oh, Grandma, I'm sorry but John couldn't come. He's still on the road. The sales trip took longer than he had planned. And I would have waited until next week but I didn't want you to be disappointed, especially since it is your birthday," and the old woman saw that Melanie held a bakery box tied with string in her hands.

Wasting her money, thought the old woman. It would be cheaper to make the cake herself, and then said aloud, "You shouldn't have come by yourself," letting her into the house. "What if something had happened to you while you were driving? What about the child? My grandson should never have let you go off on your own. Too much independence—that's what's wrong with marriages these days!" She shut and latched the door behind the young woman, not noticing the tightening of Melanie's lips nor the conscious effort she made to smile before turning back to face her husband's grandmother.

"Oh, Grandma, women are different now. We can do lots of things. And besides," she teased, "aren't you the same woman who traveled from Europe to America all by yourself?"

"That was different," the old woman answered shortly as she led the way into the small living room where she carefully sat down in her old wooden rocker. "There was a war."

Just three days after she was finally able to leave to join her husband, her parents and younger brother were killed when their little village was invaded. And by the time the news had traveled from all the way to her new home in America, the war was over, and she was expecting her first child, with only her husband beside her. "Mama!" she had cried, when the pains came. But only her husband answered.

"Grandma, did you ride on a *boat?*" Little Jennifer leaned on the arm of the rocker, stopping its rhythmic motion. She didn't know anybody who rode on a boat. Everyone she knew flew in airplanes or rode in cars when they went away. Nobody took a boat. "Was it a big boat?"

"Sit down, child. I can't rock with you leaning like that," the old woman said irritably, and the child obediently sat on the floor directly in front of the rocker, her blue eyes still fixed on the old woman's face. "Yes, it was a big boat—not that I saw much of it. We were all crowded together because there wasn't much space, and people were sick and babies were crying and the food—what little there was of it—was rotten and cold."

A young woman from the next village —one baby in her arms and an older child, crying with exhaustion and fear, at her feet—dropped down on the bench beside her. "We go to America," *she had said, pronouncing the words with reverence. Her face, though drawn with weariness, was filled with an inner serenity that shone like a candle in the dark.* "In America, I find work and my children will be strong and healthy," *and unconsciously her arms tightened around the bundle she held.* "In America, there is no war."

But two days later, the baby died, still held in its mother's arms. And by the time the boat docked at Ellis Island, the older child had grown silent, sick with some disease and past crying. By then, the young mother's face had lost its serenity and her tears fell unceasingly, like the rain that obscured the first sight of Manhattan from the immigrants' hopeful eyes.

For weeks afterward, the mother's face had haunted her, and she would wake from sleep with her tears wet on her cheeks. It could so easily have happened to her, she thought. Grief and pain were always out there, waiting to find a victim.

"I'd like to go on a boat ride," the child chattered, looking up at her mother. "Could we go sometime, Mommy?"

"Someday, sweetheart," Melanie answered absently, her eyes on the old woman's face. "But it won't be like Grandma's trip. That was different."

The old woman was silent, not hearing the conversation between the two. It had been a long time since she recalled the trip—all the hardship, the fear, the pain—or thought about that young girl who had set off with a heart full of hope. Where did she go? Did she find what she wanted?

"Grandma," Melanie interrupted gently, "why don't we have some cake now? Jennifer has been practicing to sing to you, and the cake is really something special to see."

When she ordered it, she told the bakery to decorate it with lots of icing flowers and bows. "It's for my husband's grandmother—her eighty-eighth birthday," she had explained. "I want it to be beautiful. She's been kind of depressed lately and I want to make this day as special as possible."

Sometimes, Melanie wondered if John's grandmother was ill. Other times, she thought perhaps the old woman was just lonely. But what could *they* do? They lived too far away to visit more than once a month. And even though Melanie always brought her a gift, she was wise enough to know that objects couldn't take the place of people. In any case, she was determined to make this day memorable, especially since her husband couldn't be there.

The bakery had done its part, with pink roses cascading down ribbons of icing and green leaves entwined along the edges. And as Melanie slipped the cake free from the box, Jennifer clapped her hands with excitement. But when the old woman approached the table, she only sniffed disapprovingly.

"Too much sugar," were her first words, followed by, "A lot of trouble for something we will just eat."

"Oh, Grandma, how often does an eighty-eighth birthday come anyway?" Melanie asked lightly. "And the cake is so beautiful—almost like a wedding cake" but there was no response from the old woman.

PERIPHERAL VISIONS AND OTHER STORIES

A wedding cake... hers had been small, decorated only with some fresh strawberries. There was no time and no money for a big party—not that the village would have expected it during the war. They were wed in the village church, and the next morning, he left for America, before the enemy soldiers could come and take him to fight. But she stayed behind, trying not to think of what might happen before they met again. The village could be invaded, and she could be killed, or worse, by the soldiers. Or the ship he was traveling on could sink, leaving her a widow before she had a chance to be a proper wife.

Or he could come to America and find someone smarter and prettier, someone who could make it easier for him to adjust to the loneliness. And he would forget all about the young wife he had left behind, who dressed in old-country clothes and spoke a foreign language—foreign to him because now he too was an American.

When she came, she never once asked how he had spent the long cold nights without her. She never asked, and he never said. But sometimes, after they made love, she would turn away and wonder if he was recalling someone else's arms—someone who wasn't old-country.

Melanie placed the white candles she had brought on the cake. There were eight—one for each decade—and then eight more pink ones—one for each year. As she lit them, she wondered what was on the old woman's mind. She was different somehow, as sharp-tongued as ever, but every now and again unusually quiet as though lost in memories.

Perhaps she was getting senile, she worried. Maybe we will have to bring her to live with us, and at the thought, her heart sank. She had a fondness for the old woman, not having a grandmother of her own, but she was afraid that living together would pose more problems than it solved. The old woman was quick with her criticisms and impatient with Jennifer's exuberance.

Melanie wished she could say something or do something to make the connection stronger between the two of them, but no matter how hard she tried, she wasn't able to establish a rapport with the old lady—not like John. All her husband had to do was walk into the room and his grandmother's face lightened with love. The old woman had said once that John looked like his grandfather—the same tall posture, tender brown eyes, quicksilver smile that, even after eight years, made Melanie's heart quicken.

If John were here, the atmosphere would be different. His grandmother would be less likely to find fault, perhaps be, if not warm, then at least more accepting of her granddaughter-in-law, and just more *present* in the moment.

Maybe it's her age, Melanie thought as she lit the last candle. I suppose when I'm that old, I'll drop out of conversations and my grandchildren will think I've gone senile, too. And she smiled to herself, finding it almost impossible to imagine being old.

She straightened a dripping candle more firmly in its holder, and then pulled out two chairs—one for her daughter, already rushing to her seat, and the other for the old woman.

The child held out her hands encouragingly.

"Come on, Grandma," she said excitedly. "You sit here and Mommy and I will sing and then," she paused dramatically, "I'll help you blow out the candles!"

"There's wax dripping on the cake," the old woman protested, but Jennifer began to sing, her mother's voice joining hers. Then, without even waiting, the child leaned forward and puffed out her cheeks before releasing all her breath in a gentle wind over the flames.

The candles wavered and then went out, and Jennifer clapped her hands in triumph.

"Now the present!" she shouted, slipping down from the chair to run out to the car, bringing in a flat box topped with a red ribbon and bow.

"I hope you like it," Melanie said, suddenly unsure about her choice. A pair of bedroom slippers and a warm robe would have been more suitable, she thought. But when she saw the carved wooden platter in an antique store, she had to buy it, even though it was not the kind of gift she had ever brought the old woman before.

John's grandmother lifted the lid and gazed in silence at the tray. Carved from maple, it had a raised design of grapes and leaves around the edges, painted in glowing green and purple tones. It was the most beautiful piece of carving she had seen since she had left her village.

Melanie didn't know—how could she, for the old woman rarely talked of her childhood—but her father had been a craftsman of wood, the best woodcarver for miles around. His hands could take a block of oak or pine or maple and turn it into a work of art, with life and beauty gleaming from the softly polished grain.

Her father's artistry had been responsible for her future husband's arrival in the village. He had come as an apprentice to her father, gaining not only a trade but the daughter's heart as well.

And his wedding gift to his bride had been a wooden platter, deeply carved and handsomely polished.

"In America, there will be more food than you can fit onto this platter," he had promised. "It will overflow with meat and cheese and vegetables. You will not go hungry when you live with me," he said proudly.

But when she came, it was without the platter. Along with what little else she owned, it had been sold to pay for her passage to America.

"Grandma?" Melanie said hesitantly, and the old woman realized she had been silent too long, her fingers absently tracing the deeply carved pattern the way a lover might trace the curves of his beloved's face.

"Beautiful," she murmured finally, her voice cracking as though it had been a lifetime since she had last spoken. "Thank you, child." And she reached up to pull the young woman closer so she could kiss her cheek, surprising them both into silence, while the child watched.

"Grandma," Jennifer said finally, when it seemed the grown-ups had forgotten all about the lovely cake, "do you want your cake on the new dish Mommy bought you?"

Melanie laughed, her voice catching a bit in her throat as she spoke. "Oh, sweetie, that would be too big for Grandma's piece, I think," but the old woman shook her head.

"What a good idea," and she settled herself back in the chair, while Melanie cut the first slice and then set it before her. "When I was a little girl, we had birthday parties too, but not with presents like you children have now. Our village was poor, so we would all gather together and have a meal and that was how we celebrated birthdays. Weddings, too."

Her voice was soft, almost as though she was talking to herself, or the young girl she had once been.

"I was married in the afternoon in our village church, and after, we had a wedding feast. Everyone came, even though we were all frightened of the war. But a wedding was something to celebrate, after all.

"I had long hair then," she continued, her cake untouched on the platter as she reached up almost unconsciously to stroke her gray strands. "It fell past my shoulders, and when I washed it, I would squeeze lemons over it, so it smelled of golden sunshine even in the darkness. I can still remember the scent of those lemons...."

NANCY CHRISTIE

ICE CREAM SUNDAY

"A small vanilla cone, please." It was finally his turn at the counter. For twenty minutes, Eddie had waited behind irritated parents and excited children, all the while glancing anxiously at his car. She was still there, solid and unmoving, lost in her own world.

Thank God, he thought. He was not up to chasing her today—or any day, for that matter. Once before, when his wife Millie had been ill, he had to go alone to that place to fetch her. But when they stopped for a red light, the girl had escaped. Worried, embarrassed and more than a little angry, he had to pull off and run after her—heart pounding, face sweating. She was very fast. He almost didn't catch her.

Since then, whenever he had her in the car, Eddie would fasten her seatbelt with the top side turned inwards where her clumsy fingers couldn't find the release.

"Sugar cone or plain?" The impatient voice of the young clerk brought him back to the present.

Sugar cone or plain? Which did Millie choose? She always handled these details. His wife had handled everything concerning the child. All he had to do was drive the car and pay the bills. And listen to Millie cry in the night for her lost daughter.

"Mister, sugar cone or plain?"

"Uh, sugar, I guess," and he turned back to see her leaning forward now, her stick-straight hair hiding her face. She's probably playing with the radio buttons, he thought resignedly.

She liked to turn the volume up very loud until the sound rattled the windows and crashed against his eardrums.

"You see, Eddie, she likes the music. Could she be as backward as they say if she likes the music?" His wife's anxious words echoed in his mind. Millie never let go of the hope that the doctors were wrong in their diagnosis—that somewhere, underneath all those layers of unresponsive brain cells, lurked a child ready to learn, able to love.

Eddie knew better. He knew there was nothing there, that her brain was as vacant as the look in her eyes. Their daughter—the one he and Millie longed for—was somewhere else, with some other family. And in her place was this heavy body and empty mind.

"Sir, excuse me. Would you step aside, please?" It was the boy again. He wanted Eddie to move, so he could wait on the mother and father and their two giggling golden-haired daughters.

He had never heard her laugh, he realized. The girl would sit for hours, impassive and unreachable, twirling one end of her hair or endlessly stroking the material of her dress. But she rarely made any noise at all.

Except when she was eating. "Then," he had said with disgust the first and last time they took her to a restaurant, "she sounds like a pig at a trough! I knew it was a mistake!"

At first Millie didn't answer, but busied herself gently wiping the girl's face and hands clean of the food. Then she turned to face him, with a look of disappointment in her eyes that shamed him.

"Anna's our daughter, Eddie. It's not her fault she was born this way."

It wasn't his fault either, he had wanted to answer. But he kept his peace. And it wasn't his fault that he couldn't feel a spark of affection for her. He had tried to, God knows, but as she grew older and more out of reach, he found the effort harder to maintain.

Finally, he had left it to Millie to love the girl. If he felt any sorrow at all, it was from watching his wife struggle against the reality that was their child. She was a good woman. She should have had a healthy baby, one with laughing eyes and eager smiles.

But he had done the best he could. When she grew older, he found a place that could keep her. And after Millie died—has it been six months already?—the staff expected little of him in the way of contact. He paid for the girl's care and bought what little necessities she required, but made no attempt to see her.

"It wasn't like she would know me anyway," he had explained to the nurse on duty. "Besides, what if I take her somewhere and she gets, you know, crazy? I'm an old man. I can't handle her."

It was different when Millie was alive. Then, every Sunday afternoon, they would drive out to the facility to visit her. (Millie called it "the place." She hated their daughter living behind locks and bars.) And when the weather turned warm, they would take her out for an ice cream cone.

Eddie drove, and Millie and the girl (when had he stopped thinking of her by name?) would sit in the back. Millie would carefully feed her spoonfuls of the white frozen cream, gently wiping her lips and chin after each mouthful.

"A dollar even, sir," It was the boy again, holding a cone already dripping in the heat. The outside temperature had risen unexpectedly high for early May. Maybe that was what decided him to go out for ice cream today with the girl. On such a warm day, he knew Millie would have wanted to take her out for a cone.

But there was just the two of them now, no Millie to help. And the ice cream would melt much faster than she could eat it. Even now, as Eddie watched, the drops of cream accumulated on the counter, adding to the sticky mess left by other customers.

How would he manage? he wondered, thinking of how slowly she ate. She would roll each spoonful from one side to the other inside her mouth while dribbles of white escaped from the corners of her closed lips until, finally, she swallowed.

She would smile, he remembered. Smile, and then open her mouth for another taste.

"Here," he said as he handed over the bill. "Could I have a dish? And a spoon," he added, not caring about the exasperated sigh that escaped the boy. Okay, maybe he should have thought of it before but he couldn't think of everything! Millie usually went inside and got the treat. Millie usually did it all. All he had to do was drive.

"Here's your dish. *And* your spoon. Anything else?" The heavy sarcasm was wasted on Eddie, who saw the girl trying to open the car door. He grabbed the cone and dish, shoved the spoon into the soft cream, and hurried to the door. He had to stop her before she got out. She would run, and he was too old to catch her. She would disappear—and for a split second, he saw a future with no girl to deal with. Just his life and his memories of Millie.

Only for a second, and then he was at the door, holding it closed, telling her to "Sit down! Let go!" feeling ashamed in front of all the other parents—parents with normal children.

Then, for the first time, he looked at her—really looked at her—and saw tears running down her face from her wide-open eyes. Her eyes, he realized, were the same color as Millie's, blue and clear.

"Here, what's wrong?" and Eddie set the cone in the dish, placing it carefully on the roof of the car. Gently, he opened the door. He had never seen her cry. If she did, if Millie knew, he was never told. He wouldn't have wanted to know, he thought. He had shut out all thoughts of the child and left it to Millie to do what was necessary. Like love her, he understood now. Millie had loved her the way she was, just as she had loved him, despite his faults.

He fumbled awkwardly with the seatbelt and then released the catch, and the girl turned all the way around, bumping her knee against the dashboard. She was a big girl—a woman, Eddie realized. She must be nearly forty by now.

She was staring at the backseat, looking for God knows what, he thought. Then he knew, and his throat tightened.

"Come on," and not caring what the other people thought, Eddie pulled her gently from the front seat and guided her into the back.

"Sit here," he said, as though she could understand him. That was how Millie always talked to her—as though someday she would answer.

Then, he picked up the ice cream and climbed in next to her, turning sideways so he could see her face.

"I brought you some ice cream, Anna," he said now. Dipping the plastic spoon into the sticky sweetness, he brought it to her lips.

"Try some." And gently, Eddie fed his daughter.

NANCY CHRISTIE

PANDORA'S BOX

Disjointed and incomplete, the dream stayed in my mind long after waking. A large, deep lake, and two people silently moving underwater as though they were on dry land toward an edge that led to a dark, unfathomably deep drop-off. Before them waited a large boulder (something from the Ice Age, perhaps?), and when they reached it, still silent, they rolled it toward the edge of the undersea precipice, pushing it until it fell down into the depths. Then, still not speaking, they walked back through the water until they reached the shore.

I awoke thinking about rocks and boulders and heavy objects pushed into the depths, falling into the darkness, buried where no one can find them except the two people responsible for their disappearance and perhaps even their existence. No one, that is, except an innocent, inquisitive child.

#

When I was a child, I stumbled across a trunk, pushed far back into a darkened corner of the attic. At the time, we lived in an old farmhouse, and unlike modern homes with drop-down stairs leading to unfloored areas, this house boasted an attic with ten-foot-high raftered ceilings, oak floorboards and dirt- and web-encrusted windowpanes. Often, I would climb the stairs to the second floor, pull open the heavy, dark door next to the linen closet and then mount the twisting, turning, narrow staircase that led to the attic.

PERIPHERAL VISIONS AND OTHER STORIES

This was my hiding place, my refuge. I don't know if I knew even then what it was I was hiding from or looking for. When you are raised in an environment of extreme cold, do you know with any degree of certainty that a warmer clime exists? But I knew there were times when it was better to be unseen and unseeing, unheard and unhearing.

I would take my doll and my patchwork blanket and sit next to the window, measuring the extent to which the spider's web had grown, while I waited for that indefinable moment when it was safe to return to the world I had left behind.

On that day—the day I found the trunk—the wind, rattling through a crack in the pane, had destroyed the web. Robbed of my usual routine, I began casting about for something else to occupy my attention. There were cardboard cartons, taped securely closed, and long dress bags, holding out-of-season and undoubtedly out-of-style dresses. It was behind one of those that I found the trunk, bound with leather straps that had deteriorated from the temperature extremes common to poorly insulated spaces.

I ran my fingers across the top, oddly free of dust, and then carefully lifted the lid. The first layer consisted of yellowed tissue paper, but when I pushed it aside (carelessly, like any other inquisitive eight-year-old) I found a layette resting beneath. Tiny blue booties with a cap to match, soft cotton gowns with incredibly tiny buttons, softer-still blankets and crib sheets—everything a newborn could desire, and all in shades of blue, from robin's egg to midnight.

For a boy baby, I realized, and having no brothers—indeed, being an only child—I was mystified.

And then, being a child, a child with a doll who had only one dress to her name and that one torn and dirty, I did what any child would do. I seized the nearest baby gown and ran downstairs to where my parents sat in silence in the small living room.

"Can I have this?" I asked excitedly. "It would fit Abby and she would look so pretty in it!"

I was a child, but even at that age, the deeper silence that followed my words told me that I had said something, *done* something, so wrong, so incredibly dangerous to the tenuous peace of the household, that there would be no going back.

"Where did you find that?" my father asked finally, his voice quiet but with a harsh undercurrent that caused me to move closer to my mother.

"Upstairs. In the attic," but my words had barely left my mouth before they were drowned out by my father's voice, thick with anger as I had never heard it before.

"Get that out of here! Do you hear me? Throw it out! You told me," he turned to my mother who hadn't moved yet seemed somehow to have left the room, "you told me you had gotten rid of everything! Everything! After all that happened—and still you lied to me!"

My mother rose then and took the baby gown from my grasp while I stood there, rooted to the spot, not knowing what to do. She held it gently, as though it still clothed an infant, and met my father's eyes in silence.

I must have left the room at some point. Or perhaps my father left first. Children's minds have a way of erasing events that are incomprehensible to them. All I know is that, the next time I climbed the stairs to the attic, the trunk was gone.

But its disappearance left a gap, not only in the space behind the stored clothes but also in the relationship between my parents, a chasm deeper than the one that already existed. After that day, there were long periods of silence and, when they did speak, it was with a formality that only underscored the emotion beneath the surface: his, an unyielding anger and hers, a hopeless withdrawal.

A few years later, my mother grew sick. Pale and weak, she took to spending days in her bed, and then weeks in the hospital. I didn't know then what was wrong with her—the word "cancer" was never spoken in my hearing—but I knew my mother was leaving me, breath by breath.

When there was nothing left to do for her, the doctors sent her back home, with a box of increasingly stronger pills and potions. I would come home from school, have an afternoon snack of milk and peanut butter thinly spread on crackers, and then go into her room.

"I did well on the English test," I would report or "The teacher said she hopes you are feeling better."

My mother would nod her head, as though even the exertion of forming words in her mind and then sending them to her lips was too much for her. Then she would close her eyes—the signal for me to leave the room to study or play outdoors or wait for the neighbor lady who had taken over the household tasks of cooking dinner and washing clothes.

One day, however, I had bigger news to report than a scholastic achievement.

"Momma, it happened today. The school nurse said I was to be sure to tell you. She gave me what I needed but said that I would need to get more. She said it would happen again every month from now on and I would have to wear them."

The nurse, aware of the home situation, had explained to me what was happening to my body, why there was blood where there had been none before. And she had taken great pains to reassure me that nothing was wrong, that this was normal.

My mother opened her eyes at the news, and I took heart in her interest. "She said that it was normal, that there was nothing wrong. She said," I finished proudly, "that I was a young lady now!"

I twirled around the room, stopping close to my mother's bed. She was crying, I suddenly realized. But why? Was she worried about me? Didn't she understand? Did she think I was sick?

"It's okay, Momma," I said hurriedly, trying clumsily to wipe the tears from her cheeks. "The nurse said it was okay. She said it meant I could have babies when I grew up," but there I stopped, the picture of the trunk with baby clothes suddenly filling my mind.

"No," I thought I heard my mother say, and I drew closer. "Better not to have it, better not to have children" she muttered, turning her head from side to side and then drawing in her breath sharply, as the pain, never far away, reached out for her with sharp-clawed fingers.

I poured her a glass of water and gave her the oval green pill as I had been instructed and then watched anxiously as she swallowed. I could almost trace the pill's descent down that narrow, pale column. She had grown so thin that her skin was almost translucent, so weak that the act of swallowing took all her strength, and afterward, she lay there, eyes shut and breathing ragged.

PERIPHERAL VISIONS AND OTHER STORIES

Any other time I would have waited there in silence, not daring to bother her. But something, the change in my role from child to maturing young woman, pushed me to ask a question that I never realized had waited there to be voiced.

"Whose clothes, Momma? Whose clothes were in the trunk? Did I have a brother?"

I thought for a moment she was going to tell me, but then we both heard my father's footsteps on the flagged path outside the front door and she remained silent.

Later that evening, I had come downstairs to say goodnight but stopped near the doorway to her room. My parents were talking, and it struck me then, with an awareness that I had not had before, how little they communicated—not just since her illness but for as long as I had known them. My father, not an emotionally giving person, spent his evenings in the house wrapped in silence, but I had thought all fathers were like that. And my mother, though good to me, had always maintained a distance, as though protecting herself from any further hurt.

"Promise me," and though my mother's voice was weakened from pain and medication, it carried a strength I had never heard before. "I have never asked for anything since that day, Richard, but promise me this much. It was my child!"

"Yes, it was *your* child," he said, the heaviness in his voice overlaid with a mixture of righteousness and anger. "Your child, but not mine! And now, after all this time, you think you have the right to ask me for such a thing? You have *no* right—not after what you did!"

Somehow I knew it wasn't me they were speaking of. I stood there, still as a statue, waiting and listening

"And I paid for my mistake," my mother responded wearily. "I lost everything when he died—even the child he left me. Could I not be laid to rest close by my baby, my child, my only son? I am dying, Richard. Can you not grant me just this one thing?"

I turned then, and went back upstairs. I didn't wait to hear my father's answer. I had heard far more than my young mind could take in.

Days later, my mother died, alone in the night, with no one beside her. The day of the funeral, I refused to go to the cemetery. I suppose people thought I couldn't bear to see her buried, to have to recognize that she was gone.

That wasn't it. She had left me long before she drew her last breath. What I couldn't endure was to see the outcome of my father's decision. I was certain he had not honored her dying wish and equally convinced that the refusal would haunt her, keeping her from rest.

"I'm not going," I said, while he stood in the doorway, unfamiliar in his black suit. My father was a flannel-shirt-and-overalls man and to see him so dressed up only underscored the change in our life.

"Get dressed and come downstairs," he answered, but I kept on turning the pages of my book until he finally left the room.

I didn't cry, not then and not in the long days that followed. Instead, my emotions—grief at my loss, anger at my father and, even more damaging, my own sense of guilt for causing that last final breakdown between my parents—formed an unbreakable wall of ice between the two of us.

All through the following long years, while my father and I lived in the same house, an uneasy silence existed between us. He paid the bills and gave me money for high school expenses and I dutifully handled the housework and my school responsibilities. We never spoke of my mother. What was there to say?

I knew he visited my mother's grave. Once a week he would come home with a small bouquet of flowers and the next day they were gone, no doubt placed in the metal holder at the head of her burial plot. But I never went there myself. My sense of guilt for the scene I had caused so long ago as strong as my anger at my father for denying her dying wish.

When I turned eighteen, I went away to college, then took a job on the west coast several hundred miles from home—far away from the cold Ohio winters, far enough to make visits home an inconvenience. The contact between us dwindled to the occasional phone calls as I continued to distance myself from the man whom I blamed for causing my mother so much pain.

He had refused to forgive her, I told myself. And I was his daughter. I could withhold forgiveness as well.

But ever mindful of my duty, I would call him from time to time, avoiding the word "Dad" by simply saying my name when he answered the phone. And when I married, I sent him a copy of the announcement in the paper. Although my husband was aware that my father was living, he didn't question his absence at the small ceremony. Intuitively, he sensed that this was a family matter that would not bear much questioning—that the wall I had erected was protecting me from emotions I couldn't bear to acknowledge.

But when the doctor called to tell me my father had cancer and was not expected to live much longer, Paul told me it was time to go to him.

"Your anger is eating at you, like the cancer is eating at him," he said quietly, his arms around me to keep me from leaving the room and the conversation. "Not for his sake but your own, you need to face this. You need to face him." He turned me around to look at him. "You need to forgive him, to make some kind of peace with him. He may have changed. He may regret what he did. You two may still be able to—"

"To what?" I asked, twisting free of his hands. "To fall into each other's arms and say how much we love each other? For him to say he was sorry that he hurt my mother? For me to say how sorry I was that I found that damned trunk, that I ever brought those clothes downstairs, that I caused—" and the tears I had been holding in all those years broke through.

I could see once again the pain in my mother's eyes, could hear the pleading in her voice, and could feel the implacable anger, the icy-cold weight of unforgiveness that drove my father to refuse her last request.

Paul held me—I could always count on him to give me what I needed even if I wasn't sure myself—until I was able to get my emotions under control. And then he went to the phone and made reservations for me to fly out the next day back to the town where I grew up—back to that house where my mother died and where now my father waited his turn.

But if Paul had hopes that this would lead to a deathbed reconciliation, I had none. Nothing would be different, nothing would change, I thought to myself on the ride to the house, just like nothing much had changed here. I looked out the taxi's window at the empty fields where corn stalks once stood tall and green. Everything was still the same.

The January cold pierced the shell of the cab, and even with the heater on, I shivered in the draft. Years of living in the southern California sun had made me unable to adapt to Ohio's bitter temperatures, and, as he turned the heater fan up higher, the white-haired driver broke the silence between us.

"You here for a visit?"

"Yes, just for a few days," hoping he would leave it at that.

"Me, I've been here almost all my life," he went on, garrulous as old people tend to be, "and been driving a taxi for almost forty years now. Not much call for cabs though, except with the old folks who don't drive anymore. But you're young—you don't have to worry about that," and he winked in the mirror at me.

"Mmm," I murmured, hoping he would take my lack of response as an indication that I didn't want to talk.

But he continued. "Yep, with that crowd it's a regular route: trips to doctors' offices and grocery stores, church on Sunday and then out to the cemetery to check on the graves." He turned down the street leading to my father's house, not missing a beat. "Down this road, now, there's an old guy. Every day for the past eight years I would take him to his wife's grave. I tried to talk to him but he was quiet coming and going—like you," and then he glanced down at the address I had given him. "Oh," clearly embarrassed," I didn't know you knew him," stopping in front of the house.

"It doesn't matter. I don't really know him, not really," In a way it was true.

I got out, taking my small overnight case with me, and handed him his fare. "I'll need a ride again in a few hours. Can you come back around three?"

"Sure," he said hastily. "No problem. I'll just pull up and wait for you."

I knocked at the wooden front door, noticing the peeling paint and tarnished handle, and waited for the visiting nurse to let me in. My father, the doctor had told me, was too ill to be left alone without any supervision.

"I'm glad you were able to come," the woman said, no judgment in her voice. She took my coat and said, "I just put on a pot of coffee. Why don't you have some and I can bring you up to date," and obediently, willing to delay the inevitable, I followed her into the kitchen.

"It won't be long now. I've seen this before," she said matter-of-factly. "They may rally for a few days but then the end comes. The pain patch is working well enough although he still has periods where I need to give him morphine, too." Nothing in her voice indicated that she thought it odd that a daughter should need to be informed as to her own father's status. I set down my empty cup and she asked, "Do you want to go in now?"

"Is he sleeping?" hoping that, if I dragged out the conversation, he might die without my having to face him.

"No, he's awake. He knows you were coming," she added, and then stood. "Come along," the way a mother might encourage a child to face some dreaded task: a test, perhaps, or a doctor's visit.

He lay in the room where my mother had died, and at first, the sound of the oxygen machine was all I could hear. But then, he cleared his throat and the nurse moved to give him a sip of water from a nearby glass.

"Your daughter is here, Richard," and she helped shift his head so he could better see me where I stood.

He looked at me, his eyes squinting against the light, but I couldn't tell if he knew who I was.

He closed his eyes again—Too tired? In dismissal?—and the nurse led me from the room. "Why don't you go upstairs and rest a bit? You've had a long trip. I've put you in your parents' room. I hope you don't mind, but I've been sleeping in your room. It was closer to the stairs in case he called me during the night."

My parents' bedroom had always been off limits to me, I don't know why, and I half-expected to hear one of them tell me to go back to my own room. But there was only silence—no one to reprimand me, no one to care what I did or suffer the consequences of my actions.

One by one, I pulled open the drawers, first checking the dresser where my mother's flannel nightgowns and serviceable underwear still waited in neat stacks, and then the highboy, where my father kept his clothes. When my search yielded nothing, I turned to the closet, pulling the cord attached to the single bulb to shed some light on the darkness. And that was when I saw it—the same small trunk that was once hidden in the attic, now stowed under my mother's dresses and my father's pants.

I slid the trunk forward and opened it, seeing, as I did so many years before, the blue booties and cap, the soft gowns and blankets. Paying closer attention, I could see the fine stitching, the embroidery on the blanket edging. These were no store-bought items, I realized, but ones handmade with great attention to detail, with care and time and love.

"When did she make these?" I wondered aloud, fingering the fine soft material, slipping my hand underneath the blanket to feel the warmth. I thought back but couldn't remember my mother being pregnant—even a child would notice the swelling, the change in the shape of a woman's body.

So, it had happened before I was born. There was certainly plenty of time, since my mother was in her early forties before I came along, even though she married my father right before the Korean War when she was barely twenty, just a few months before he shipped out. The child, I realized, must not have been my father's. While he was off fighting in the war, my mother must have had an affair, and the outcome of it was a baby who lived just a short time yet long enough to inexorably alter the landscape of their marriage.

That would explain his anger when I bought the baby clothes downstairs that day. Unwittingly, I had reopened old wounds that had never healed but instead festered under the surface. How many times had she secretly visited the attic, brushing the dust from the lid of the trunk before taking out the baby clothes? I imagined her caressing the gowns, holding the blankets to her heart as she grieved for the child who was gone from her, before going back downstairs to the life she had now.

It didn't matter, I told myself, as I pushed the trunk back into the closet. So she made a mistake—was that a reason to punish her all those years? But if he did hate her, I wondered, why keep the trunk with its incriminating layette after she died? Did he want some tangible reminder of her infidelity?

Or did he feel some guilt for how he had treated her at the end? "*That* was what they were arguing about," I said aloud, recalling that last conversation. She had wanted the baby to be buried by her, in the plot she and my father had purchased years ago. But his anger was so strong that he couldn't even agree to her last request.

But *I* could, I realized now. He was no longer in a position to interfere and maybe if I did this one last thing for my mother, she would forgive me for the pain I had caused.

I heard the clock strike three. The taxi would be waiting to take me to meet Father John at the cemetery. But instead of one burial I would be arranging two—moving the child's body to lie next to my mother's.

During the short ride to the graveyard, just beyond the church, the driver kept silent, speaking only when he stopped at a section not too far from the entrance.

"This is where his wife is buried," he said, turning to face me as he pointed to a cluster of graves under a bare-limbed oak. "Or at least, that's where he always went," and then turned back, his eyes fixed on the steering wheel as I left the warmth of the car and made my way across the frozen earth.

For the first time since my mother died, I saw her grave—a single small headstone with her name and date of death marking the spot. And next to it, where I expected to see a space for my father's, a smaller marker with just a child's name—"Joseph"—and a single entry marking both his birth and death. Yet its closeness to my mother's grave made it clear to whom the long-dead infant belonged.

"Your father ordered the grave moved." I started at the sound of a voice and turned to find an elderly priest at my side.

"Father John from St. Mary's," and he held out his hand to me. "I didn't mean to intrude but I like to keep an eye on the graveyard. Sometimes the teenagers..." and he let his voice drop off expressively. "And I knew who you were, of course," adding, at my questioning look, "You look so much like your father—the same stern face, the same gray eyes."

"When did he move the grave?" I asked finally.

"When he made arrangements for his own burial some months ago. He knew he was dying, and I think he wanted to make amends before it was too late, to forgive her for what she did and perhaps to ask her forgiveness as well. You know about the baby, I take it."

"Yes," I answered, unwilling to confess my part in what had happened.

"I told your father a long time ago he should talk to you, that children often know more than adults give them credit for. But he refused. And then you left," and I heard in his voice some measure of reproach.

"I knew the whole story, of course," and the priest shook his head sadly. "They were newly married and then he had gone off to war, leaving your mother alone. I don't condone what she did but I understood it. But then, she wasn't my wife. You must not judge your mother too harshly," he added. "She was a good woman but vulnerable. And the man, well, I knew him as well. He loved your mother deeply. He went off, too—he was in the Air Force while your father was an Army man—before he knew about the baby. He never came back. I suppose he died—so many men did. Perhaps it's just as well it all worked out the way it did," he said. "The Lord knows what's best for everyone.

"You know, your father loved your mother. When he found out about the baby she had lost, he was hurt beyond belief. I would tell him he had to forgive her, that they had to make a new start. And I had hoped when you were born that maybe it wasn't too late. They had caused each other so much pain. So much misunderstanding... So many losses." He shook his head again.

He leaned forward and brushed the snow away from the headstone. "I thought for a while that they had made peace with what happened. Oh, I'm not naïve enough to think a man like your father would completely forgive and forget," and he smiled briefly. "But I had hoped that, in time, they could find their way. Then, something happened. I could tell when they came to Mass. The way they stood, never looking at each other. The silence between them when they left the church. Even in your behavior," and he looked at me. "I would watch you stand there—you were how old then? Eight? Nine?—waiting for something. I tried to talk with your father but he would have none of it. He just said I couldn't possibly understand. And your mother... well..." and his words drifted off.

It wasn't my fault, I wanted to say. I didn't create the situation. I only found the trunk—the Pandora's box that let loose the pain in the house. But I knew now, too late, that knowledge makes one a party to the situation.

He came back to the present and reached out to shake my hand. "Call me when you need me," he said, adding, "I have offered to go to your father but he left instructions that I was only to be called when... well, at the end," and again that small smile. "But I pray for him. He can't prevent that" He turned and headed back to the rectory.

I stood there a while longer, thinking of the time wasted, the opportunities lost, the words unspoken and the forgiveness withheld. It was too late now to make up for the hurt I had caused my father and myself, I thought. Or was it?

They say that when Pandora opened the box, misfortunes and sorrows were let loose to plague all of mankind. But Hope, the only good amongst so much evil, was kept safe, for Pandora had quickly closed the lid once she realized what she had done. And there it remained to be a comfort to those in pain.

I stood there until my fingers and feet were numb from the cold. Then I went back to the cab where the driver waited patiently.

"Back home?" he asked and I nodded, and then sat quietly in the back seat, not sure what I would do or say when I returned, but hoping that somehow the right words could come and we would both be released from the weight of that long-buried boulder.

PERIPHERAL VISIONS AND OTHER STORIES

LUCINDA AND THE CHRISTMAS LIST

"Is this... No, may I speak with the... No, that's not right either... Hello, my name is...."

"May I help you?" I interrupted her, certain that, wherever this obviously scripted conversation was going, I didn't want to follow. I was tired. I was hungry. And my microwave bell was signaling that my "honey-dipped chicken tenders with fragrant mashed potatoes and crisp green beans" were ready for consumption, if not quite living up to the package hype.

But then, I thought to myself as I pulled out the tray, few things do in this world.

"I'm sorry," and then came a belch of such significant proportions that I instinctively moved the phone from my ear, in case any of the breath made its way through the phone wires.

"I'm sorry," she said again. "My name is Lucinda and this is really my first day on the job and even though I went through a lot of training—six months starting last July!—I don't think practice is the same as real life, know what I mean?"

"May I help you?" I said again, rummaging through the drawer for a clean fork or spoon. Obviously I needed to wash dishes since all twenty-three of my mismatched eating utensils were at that moment sitting in the sink with dried bits of food stuck all over them.

"Anyway, I'm calling to ask you if you have made your Christmas list yet because—"

"Look, please take my name and number off your list. I already gave at the office."

This was a lie in more ways than one. For one thing, I hadn't given anything anywhere yet—not a dime into the red kettles, not a dollar into the food pantry collection baskets. It wasn't that I was selfish or cheap or uncaring but rather because I just hadn't gotten around to it yet.

I'd do it as soon as I had a few extra bucks, I would tell myself every time I passed by one of the opportunities to "give so everyone can have a Merry Christmas," as one of the signs proclaimed. It was just that, so far, I didn't have any hard currency to spare.

As for the "office" part—that was just a repurposed utility closet off my kitchen where I managed to eke out a living editing theses and manuscripts and résumés for people who needed my creative touch and ability to identify the proper usage of the possessive and plural form of nouns. And the only money I had "donated" thus far was the monthly rent check to my landlord.

"I'm not asking for anything," she said, her chipper voice starting to grate on me. "Well, that's not true. I *am* asking for something but what I am asking for is your *list*. Your *Christmas* list. According to our records, you haven't submitted one yet and if we don't get it in time, there's a chance that your delivery will be delayed. After all, it *is* December 23rd."

"Oh, for—look, I don't know *who* you are or *what* you want but my dinner is waiting for me," I said, opening another drawer in search of any plasticware that would work in a pinch. I was hungry and my meal, such as it was, was starting to cool.

"Third drawer down," she said, and without thinking I moved to open the one she had suggested and then stopped in mid-pull.

"What?" not sure if I had heard her right.

"Third drawer down. That's where you put the utensils you get from Mama Leonie's and Pho Ho takeaway. Papa's Pizzeria only gives you napkins. I guess they figure you eat your cheese-and-broccoli pizza with your hands, so why waste the inventory?"

That was more than a little weird. How did *she* know where I ordered my meals? Was this yet another indication of personal information being sold to the highest bidder, namely the telemarketing industry? Or was I being *spied* on?

I instinctively closed the blinds over the kitchen sink, went to the living room where I pulled the curtains shut and then checked to make sure my front door was still triple-locked.

"I'm sorry, I'm doing this all wrong. My instructor told me if I wasn't careful, I'd scare people and that's just what I did. Let me try again. My name is Lucinda and—"

"What do you want?" I intended to make my voice belligerent and demanding, but instead it came out all quavery.

"We need that list," she said. "When you were a child, you were very good about putting it together early enough that we could access it, even if most of the items you requested weren't really within our power. And we really felt bad about that, especially the one for a real horse. That was on your list every year from when you were five until you were ten. But we did bring you the Suzy doll and her pony Sassy—remember?"

This was beyond weird and into the scary category—the stuff nightmares were made of. How did she know about *that*?

"Don't worry about how I know all this," she said reassuringly. "It's just part of your file. I mean, if I wanted to, I could even tell you what you wanted during those horrible high school years when all you asked for was—"

"A face with no breakouts and a date with Billy. And I didn't get either one," I added bitterly. "Fat lot of good writing letters to Santa did me!"

"Now, don't feel that way. Besides, that's all in the past. This is a new Christmas and you still have time to write your list and check it twice so my boss can review it and bring you what you most need this holiday."

Just for a minute, I let myself fantasize what I would ask Santa for this year—that is, if Santa really did exist and if there was a chance that he was delivering presents to grown-up people who ought to know better than to have expectations.

How about some cash? Not a lot, mind you. I mean, I wouldn't ask to be the sole winner of the mega-million Powerball. Just enough so I could feel rich—even if it only lasted until I paid my bills and was broke again.

Or somebody to have a holiday dinner with. When I was a kid, the entire extended family—aunts and uncles, cousins and grandparents—came to our house for Christmas Eve. We stuffed our faces with way too much of my Aunt Carol's breaded chicken and ate way too many of my mother's spicy gingerbread cookies before heading off to midnight Mass where Grandpa usually nodded off and my grandmother had to keep nudging him so he wouldn't snore.

But that was a long time ago, and eventually members of the older generation died and we cousins scattered from our Midwestern birthplace to the rest of the world, settling for staying in touch via the annual Christmas emails.

PERIPHERAL VISIONS AND OTHER STORIES

I had moved to an apartment in the city, where it was just me and my computer. And most of the time I didn't mind living alone. But every December, when the grocers had signs advertising "Buy now for your holiday dinner!" and the bakery down the street advised people to "Get your order in now for your family's treats!" I found myself remembering those gingerbread cookies and wishing I had someone to share the Christmas Eve dinner with, even if the food was only takeout.

What else? Wasn't I supposed to come up with *three* wishes?

"No, that's for a genie. I'm not a genie. I'm one of Santa's elves." Lucinda's voice interrupted my thoughts and brought me back to reality. "Now, I won't keep you any longer, but if you could put something together by tonight, we might still be able to deliver on time. So have a good evening and we look forward to receiving your information." And before I could ask anything or say anything, the line clicked and Lucinda was gone.

I checked my caller ID, but it was of no use whatsoever. I didn't know who had called—okay, she said her name was Lucinda, but I mean I didn't know what company she was with—but the amount of intel she had on me was downright spooky. I picked at the chicken, but for some reason I just wasn't hungry anymore.

I threw away the food, and then headed back to my laptop to finish the last project I had for the year: editing a badly written novel by a guy who figured he was the next best thing in the literary world. I highlighted, red-lined and commented on just about every line in the hundred-thousand-word manuscript, printed it out, and then somewhere around midnight, shut down the system, too tired to think about writing one more thing.

But all night long, I tossed and turned, my sleep punctuated with dreams about Santa and elves named Lucinda and unfinished lists and unanswered requests. I woke up the next morning, stiff, crabby, and out of sorts, and not at all happy to see that a freezing rain was pelting my windows.

Great. Christmas Eve and the powers-that-be—namely Mr. Claus—didn't even have the decency to send some snow to create the right atmosphere. No, what we got was a bone-chilling mix of wet and wind—unpleasant enough if you were only looking out the window but even worse if you had to trudge seven blocks to the post office. Which was what I had to do, thick manila envelope in hand, since the would-be novelist demanded that I snail-mail my edits back to him.

By the time I got there, the line had snaked all the way out into the lobby, with people holding packages and rubber-banded holiday card envelopes—all of which they should have sent weeks ago to avoid the December 24th rush. After forty-five minutes, I was finally able to get rid of my envelope and pick up my own mail—all bills, I noticed—before heading out in the miserable weather, my hat pulled down over my forehead as far as it could go in a vain attempt to keep my sinuses from freezing.

Maybe that was why I didn't see him. Or maybe I was too busy thinking about last night's call and wondering if I should change my phone number. In any case, I ran right into the old man, and, in the process, dropped my batch of envelopes into a puddle of dirty water.

"Sorry," I said, and he answered, "That's quite all right," and quickly bent down to pick up my mail. For an old man, he was pretty spry, I thought as I reached out for my stuff. Not that I wanted the bills but still, it *was* my mail. And maybe he thought there were checks in there—monetary gifts to help me trim my non-existent Christmas tree—that he could take without my noticing.

"No, I just didn't want them to get any wetter," he said, holding them out but I stopped in mid-reach. Had I spoken my thoughts aloud? How *did* he know what I was thinking? "Now you'd better get going because you've got that list to finish. She's waiting for it, you know."

I grabbed my stuff and backed away. Was I in the middle of some Twilight Zone episode? I *knew* what list he was talking about—the same list Lucinda had brought up the night before. My Christmas list—the one I had no intention of writing.

"Merry Christmas!" he called after me but I didn't even answer, just hopped on the first bus that came by and stayed on until three stops past my street before I finally got off and trudged back home.

It's all in your head, I kept telling myself once I was inside the apartment, door triple-locked and blinds and curtains shut. There is no such thing as Santa Claus. But as I started sorting through the bills, the idea of a Christmas list kept nagging at me. And then I found it, in the midst of all the mail I didn't want: a small green invitation-sized envelope with just my first name on the outside and inside, an invitation to the 7th Street Mission for a Christmas Eve dinner at 7 PM.

Was it just my imagination or was there a faint aroma of ginger and cloves clinging to the paper?

"Don't forget to write your Christmas list!" was scrawled across the bottom, just above the signature: "Lucinda," written in green ink with a big red smiley face next to it.

I knew where the Mission was. It was eight blocks over and three blocks down, in what was considered to be a bad section of town. There was no way I was going there. Not tonight. Not any night. And especially not now, since I noticed that it had started to snow and snow *hard*—big fat flakes that promised a significant accumulation by morning.

But if I didn't, what would happen next? Another call or a message or, God forbid, a visit from Lucinda, my very own personal crazy holiday stalker? No, anything was better than sitting here, I told myself, as I headed back out into the cold. Besides, I might as well buy this week's dollar lottery ticket. That was my sole concession to optimism, and so far, it had proved to be a waste of four quarters.

I stopped at Hank's Newspapers, paid for my ticket, and then kept walking, all the while telling myself I should go home, as people bumped into me and the snow froze on my eyelashes. But I didn't, and before I knew it, there I was, in front of the 7th Street Mission, where a bedraggled Santa in the doorway was waving people in.

I had no intention of entering, but as I turned to head back uptown, some little kid came out of nowhere, grabbed my hand, and yanked me inside.

"C'mon," he said, pulling me. "We've been waiting forever! Mommy saved you a seat just like Lucinda said to, but we thought you'd never get here! And I'm hungry!" He pushed his way through the crowd, towing me behind him like a tugboat leading a resistant barge. And before I knew what was happening, I was shoved into an old folding chair across from a woman wearing a coat that had definitely seen better days.

"Oh, good, Paul found you!" she said, smiling as though I was her long-lost buddy. "When Lucinda was leaving, she said you'd be here but I was starting to worry."

"Lucinda?" feeling as stupid as I sounded. "She was *here*?"

"Of course," the woman said, while brushing the too-long hair out of her son's face. The kid was badly in need of a haircut, I thought. And a better shirt. And possibly a lot more food, judging by the way his wrist and collarbones were sticking out. "Lucinda is always here! Now, Paul, you can go ahead and eat," and he dug into the plate of turkey and mashed potatoes and green beans as though he hadn't eaten in days.

And maybe he hadn't, I thought, but then returned to more important matters. "So she told you I was coming," I prompted, and she stopped eating her meal long enough to answer.

"Yes. She said to save a seat for you—I'm sorry, she didn't tell me your name but she said Paul would know who you were—and that it was very important. No, that's not right—she said that you *needed* to be here. Are you—I mean, you don't have a place to stay either?"

"No, I have an apartment," I said, digging into the food that one of the volunteers had put in front of me. For a minute I felt guilty eating what was clearly intended for those people who were hungry and homeless but, what the hell, I was here and Lucinda had said I was coming so it must be all right—not even stopping to ask myself why I was willing to accept what some strange person had said. A person, by the way, that I wasn't even entirely sure existed but if she did, was pretty weird and potentially dangerous.

"How nice," and the woman looked like she meant it. "Paul and I have an apartment, too. Or at least we did, but when I lost my job at the end of November I didn't have the rent for this month and my landlord said if I didn't pay him by tonight he was going to throw our stuff out and lock the door. That's how I ended up here. Lucinda told me that I could get a good meal here and that afterward everything would be okay. But...."

She looked down, but not before I saw the tears in her eyes. She sniffed, blew her nose, and then looked over at her son who was watching her intently. "Finish your meal, sweetheart," and obediently he went back to eating, but his sidelong glances at his mother showed his concern.

"Okay, everybody," and there was Santa, sitting in an old rocking chair on the small stage. "It's time for Santa to give the kids their gifts!"

A herd of squealing short people mobbed the stage while the staff tried to get them into some semblance of a line.

"Go ahead, Paul," the woman said, but he hung back, one hand holding onto his mother's chair while the other was shoved deep into his pocket, as though to keep from reaching out. The line grew shorter, the room more littered with wrapping paper and ribbons, and still Paul waited until finally he took a chance and headed to the end of the line, followed by the last lone straggler.

"He's having a hard time with the holidays this year," his mother said, her eyes following him. "His dad died this summer. He had been sick a long time but still we hoped he could get better. And since then, Paul just doesn't expect anything good to happen. Even when he had his birthday, he refused to make a wish and blow out the candle on his cupcake. He said wishes never come true anyway. And he told me just last week that Santa was stupid, that nobody believed in him and that kids like him wouldn't get anything anyway. Maybe if he gets a present he'll believe in Santa again. You have to believe in something, you know," and she turned back to look at me. "Don't you think so? I mean, sometimes, that's all you have."

I didn't know what to say since I was more in line with her son's thinking than hers. But some response was called for so I reached into my pocket, hoping to find a couple of bucks I could give her to help with her situation. It wouldn't be much—the money I had was already earmarked for bills and stuff I needed—but at least it would be something. But all I found was the lottery ticket.

"Here," and I handed it over, adding, "It's from Santa" so she wouldn't feel like a charity case, even though she was.

"Why, thank you!" and she smiled. "I don't have anything for you, though" and she started to give it back when her son returned to the table, eyes downcast and chin quivering.

"Paul, where is your present?" she asked, and he didn't look up but just swallowed before answering.

"They said that Santa's elves must have miscounted because when we got up there—me and that other boy—there was only one present left in the bag. So I remembered how Daddy always said that we should give to others so I let him have it. But I really wanted it, Mommy! How come Santa didn't make sure there was enough for both of us?" and he burst into tears.

"Oh, baby, I'm so sorry," and she pulled him close and stroked his hair.

I sat there like an idiot, wanting to say something but at a complete loss for words. So instead I looked around for something to distract them both, and saw the lottery ticket she had dropped onto the table.

"Here, why don't you do the scratch-off?" I said, tapping the mother on the arm. "You never know," although I knew perfectly well that the odds on it being a winner were slim to none.

"Good idea," she said, and gently pushed her son off her shoulder, straightening his jacket and handing him a tissue to blow his nose. "What do you think, Paul?" and she held up the card, reading the directions aloud. "'Uncover three like numbers and you win the amount shown below the numbers. Uncover two like numbers and a gingerbread man symbol and you win five times that amount.' Come on, Paul, let's see if Santa has a surprise for us after all!"

He sat up and watched her movements, but I could tell that his heart wasn't in it, especially when the first two of the six Christmas ornaments she cleared weren't a match but a number two worth one dollar and a number eight worth ten.

"All we need are three that are the same or two matches and a gingerbread man," and I couldn't tell if she was saying it to him or to herself. She uncovered a third one to show a number three, followed by a fourth ornament also bearing the number three—each worth a thousand bucks.

She stopped for a minute, but Paul jiggled her arm. "Hurry up, Mommy, we have two of them already! Maybe we'll have one more three and we'll get the thousand dollars!"

But still she hesitated, and I knew what she was thinking. If the ticket *wasn't* a winner, then Paul would be disappointed again. And I cursed myself for giving them even just one second of hope when it would most likely be followed by despair.

"You have to believe," she murmured to herself, and scratched the second-to-last ornament. But this time it was a nine, with the two-dollar symbol below the ornament.

She waited and then took a deep breath and scratched off the last ornament face. I couldn't see what it was because she had her hand over it, trying to shield Paul from one more disappointment. But his eyes were sharp and he started yelling loud enough that you could hear his voice over the din of all the other people.

"It's a gingerbread man! It's a gingerbread man! We won, Mommy, we won!"

And he was right. They had just won five grand with the ticket I bought. Five thousand dollars. I could pay a lot of bills with five thousand dollars. I could buy a new computer and still have money left over with five thousand dollars. I could go on a vacation for the first time in years with five thousand dollars.

Just for a minute, I wanted to snatch it back—tell them that it was all a mistake and that the money was mine. But I couldn't. Not when I saw how happy Paul was. Not when I saw the relief wipe out the lines etched on her face.

Oh, what the hell. It was only money.

"Are you sure?"

I realized that the woman knew what I had been thinking and was prepared to hand it back to me if I asked for it.

"Yeah, I'm sure," and I smiled. At that moment, I felt richer than I would have had I kept the ticket.

"Oh, Paul," and she grabbed her son and hugged him. "We can pay the rent and buy some food and get you books and—" she couldn't say anything more because she was crying so hard and everyone around her was coming over to find out what had happened.

"She gave it to me and it was a winning ticket!" And she pointed to me and the people started clapping their hands and hugging me and her and Paul, and even Santa got into the act.

"She's our Christmas angel!" she said but I shook my head, uncomfortable with all the applause and accolades since after all it was just a fluke that the ticket was a winner. I mean, would I have given it to her if I had known it was worth that much money?

"Of course you would have," someone whispered in my ear, and I turned around, sure that it was Lucinda, but with all the people I couldn't see who had said it.

Then someone started singing Christmas carols and the volunteers came around with cookies and somebody else started taking pictures of the crowd, and even though it was late and I knew it was cold outside, I didn't want to leave. And then the church bells started chiming and I realized it was midnight.

"Merry Christmas!" and the mother came around the table to hug me and kiss me on the cheek. "You don't know how much your gift means to the two of us!" and she looked over at Paul, who was singing "Jingle Bells" at the top of his voice. "It's not about the money. It's about how it made Paul feel. About having hope, I mean. And that's not something you can buy, know what I mean?"

And I did. Hope and love and faith—that was all part of the holiday spirit. Not some stupid things you put on your Christmas list. And for the first time in a long time, I really felt the warmth and magic and wonder of the season.

That feeling stayed with me all the way home, and by the time I got to my apartment, I wasn't even surprised to see a tiny Christmas tree sitting in front of my door, with a red-and-green beribboned box underneath. I carried them both inside and set the tree on the table before unwrapping the package. Even before I got the lid off the box, I knew what I would find. The aroma of cinnamon, ginger and cloves was unmistakable. And there, sitting on top of the gingerbread cookies, was a photo from the night's festivities.

There I was, with Paul and his mother hugging me and the rest of the crowd gathered around as though, for that moment, we were all one big family celebrating the holiday together.

I turned it over to read the note on the back.

"Even though you didn't write it down, Santa knew what you needed this year! Merry Christmas! Love, Lucinda."

NANCY CHRISTIE

BOXING LIFE

"There are years that ask questions and years that answer"—Zora Neale Hurston

This is the year that asks questions. It must be, because I have no answers, no answers at all.

I have spent the better part of the past month packing boxes, writing directions with a fat black marker on rectangular white labels: "Put in storage room," "Put in bedroom," "Leave in garage."

I keep thinking that, if I write out enough labels and put them on enough boxes, all the scattered bits of my life will come together like some giant jigsaw puzzle pieces to form a new picture. One that is better, happier, safer than the old. One that holds the promise of tomorrow without any overshadowing threats from yesterday.

But the bottom line is that there aren't enough labels. Or enough ink in my marker. And even if there were, no one is paying close enough attention to the words I've written so carefully.

It's just as well. I have a sneaking suspicion that, despite my planning, the bedroom box will really go downstairs and the garage box will undoubtedly hold the very items I will be requiring first thing in the morning, as I stumble around the unfamiliar kitchen, looking for a cup, a spoon, a bowl.

I mold my hands around the chipped mug as I sip my sixth (seventh?) cup of coffee. Despite the calendar announcing the month as July, it's chilly in the house this early in the morning. Last night, we hit a record low of forty-nine degrees and the house still holds most of that untimely cold. I pulled your old flannel robe from your closet—the only closet I hadn't yet emptied—and now huddle in its warmth.

Do you know what I remember right now? I remember how, before you came to share my bed, I used to have to pile blankets and comforters on top of me to keep warm. I was always cold in the winter. I wore long flannel nightgowns and knee socks every night. The first night you stayed, you told me at breakfast I looked like a little girl, with my hair all whichway and my socks bunched around my ankles. And when I went to make the bed, I found that all but one of the blankets had been kicked to the floor.

I realized then that I hadn't been cold, not once, throughout that long, frozen January night. I had been warm as toast, warm as a cat's fur when she lies stretched out in the hot summer sun. Warm as a little child, held safe and secure in her mother's arms. So warm I thought never to be cold again.

Questions—this started out about questions, and the dearth of answers. Of course, I had all the typical questions: When? What happened? Why? Why me? The last, I am ashamed to say, was the one I repeated endlessly for weeks, until someone had the courage to answer, "Because! Because things happen! Because it was your turn and that's just the way it goes!"

So I stopped asking, at least out loud, and instead did all the things I was supposed to do: make coffee, make calls, make plans.

Now I am packing boxes. Most of them are gone already. I gave away so many things—things of yours, things of mine, things we had purchased together. The house is sold. The new couple will be in it tomorrow. They are a nice couple, young, with two children and a third on the way. She looks tired and he looks strained, but it's probably just the effort of moving to a new place and leaving the old one behind.

You know, you always leave a piece of yourself wherever you have been. And I have been a lot of places in these past years. I am sure, if I walked very slowly along the Lake Erie shoreline, I would find traces of my six-year-old footprints in the sand. My parents had a vacation cottage at the lake, and we used to spend weeks up there. To this day, the sound of the waves breaking on the shoreline brings back the odor of dying fish and the feel of gritty sand, the smell of my father's tobacco and the clink of the ice in my mother's old-fashioned. Late every afternoon, she would have an old-fashioned.

"Earl, I need my drink," she would say and my father would drag himself up from the hammock and fix it for her. I don't know why she didn't do it herself. She was certainly capable of it. She knew how to make, and drink, more alcoholic concoctions than any of my friends' parents did.

But she always asked my father and he always did it. And I never knew why. Questions, always questions....

But that's not what I was talking about. What *was* I talking about? Oh, yes, about leaving behind pieces of yourself. In which case, I should be but a shadow of my former self, with all those pieces lying around in the world. Or maybe arrested for littering. I can hear the judge now: "You have been charged with first degree littering and in evidence, we bring this footprint, this dog collar, this spot of blood. How do you plead?"

"Guilty, Your Honor," and I would be sentenced to search for every bit of me that was scattered far and wide. And once I found them all, I would have to glue them together until I made a life-size replica of the me-who-was-and-who-is-no-more.

Dog collar—and if she hadn't been so damned clever she wouldn't have managed to slip free of the rhinestone-studded collar I had bought with my allowance. I'd never had a pet before, and with no brothers or sisters, I was lonely. Or was I? Maybe I didn't know I was lonely. Maybe I thought everybody felt this way, as though life was one long, dark corridor filled with doors, and behind every door there was a party going on, but if you didn't know the right words—and I never did—the door wouldn't open and you would have to just keep on walking.

She was my dearest companion, too small to cause much trouble but not so small that you would think she was a dustball with legs. I would take her with me on walks along the shore, and sometimes I could even convince her to wade out a bit, just enough to get her belly soaked into cold wet points of fur. When she left the collar behind, I thought it was her way of telling me she'd be back. But she never did come back, not once the rest of that summer, and the next summer, when my father left to make old-fashioneds for someone else's mother, the trips to the lake stopped. If she did come back then, she wouldn't have been able to find me.

As for the blood, well, I expected a lot more. Veiled comments from my mother had led me to believe a veritable river of red would come gushing out and all the world would know what I had done. But the fact of the matter was, all it was just a little spot, or two, easily rinsed out of my panties. Nothing much. And, in retrospect, the event that preceded it was nothing much either.

Everybody did it back then. Doing it—"it" being, of course, the accepted term for losing one's virginity, generally in the back seat of a car—was the way through the doorway leading from innocence to knowledge. At least, that's what we thought.

"Come on come on you'll like it I'll be careful you want it I know you do" the words running together faster and faster as though the speed alone would push you to make a decision. And all the while, hands here and hands there and really, while it wasn't so great, so wonderful, so earth-shattering, it was exciting enough, dangerous enough, to make the decision so much easier.

Later, of course, while the bra was being hooked and the jeans zipped, you wondered what all the rush was for, if the act itself was going to be over in a matter of minutes. What was the hurry, you wondered, and close on the heels of that question came the others: Was it me? Didn't I do it right? Wasn't I good enough? Questions that never got answered back then, but soon, if you were lucky enough, became irrelevant in the context of the next duet.

Where was I? Oh yes, packing the boxes, labeling the boxes, sealing the boxes. Wouldn't it be nice if everything in life came in such perfectly packed boxes? "Don't open until you're sixteen and then put away in your underwear drawer." "This is for your thirty-fifth birthday." "To be opened only in case of emergency."

That's the one I need right now. A box for situations that threaten to prove overwhelming. You once said that I could handle anything. But you're wrong, you know. If I have handled everything life has thrown at me, it is only because, until now, life has been kind. It has weighed each brick on some great cosmic scale and measured it against my strength.

"Not yet," I can hear life say. "This one is just a little heavier than she can take."

Clearly this past year life took a vacation. Or maybe the scale was broken and he had to resort to guessing, squinting with one black eye closed as he hefted the brick in his bony hand. "Yeah, I think it's okay. It feels a little heavy, but you know, I've gone pretty easy on her these past couple years. Besides, I'm tired of the whole thing anyway. I think I'll just give it a good heave and consequences be damned."

I bet if the light was strong enough, I could even see the bruise where the brick hit me. It hurts like hell. Ah, well, if it had to be one of us, I guess I'm glad it's me, not you. You had it easier. They told me it was just like taking one deep breath and letting it out and then not taking another. That's what they said anyway, but what do they know? They are still breathing.

I hear the moving van out front. I suppose they want to load the boxes now and get on the road. It will be strange leaving this house where we had spent so many years together. I take one final walk-through, opening bedroom closets and checking kitchen cabinets for forgotten items.

Did I pack all the memories? Or would it be wiser to leave some, to reduce their painful weight to manageable proportions? But if I did that, what part of me would also be left behind?

Questions, always questions... and with them, the hope there is enough of me safely packed away in all these boxes to go on.

NANCY CHRISTIE

THE FLOWERBED

Margaret lay still and silent on her narrow bed, listening to the sounds from the floor below. After so many years, she could picture his actions as clearly as though she was there, watching him.

There was the sound of the key in the lock, Frank fumbling a bit—was it the alcohol that blurred his vision, Margaret wondered, making it harder for him to focus on the narrow brass opening? The door opened and slammed shut again, and the slithering noise that followed meant he had failed once again to hang his heavy work coat on the old-fashioned coat rack.

Then, a muttered expletive as he located and switched off the small light she had left burning—as much for him as for herself. Those nights he stayed late at the bar: without a light, he would someday stumble and fall down the narrow staircase leading upstairs.

And in the morning—it was so dark when she arose, too early for even the sun to light the cold house—she could use the light to guide her steps as she came down to make Frank's coffee.

He knew she needed the light. That was why he shut it off, risking his own neck in the process. He didn't like money wasted, and her safety and comfort were not reason enough to spend precious pennies for electricity.

There were other small economies Frank insisted on, making Margaret's life more difficult and harsh than necessary.

Her grocery budget was so restricted that all she could afford were the cheapest cuts of meat.

Still listening to the sounds below, she ran her tongue over her teeth, able to taste the greasy film left by the meatloaf she had made for dinner. The butcher must have given her the pound of hamburger with the most fat and gristle.

Frank would have hated tonight's dinner had he come home. But he had gone straight from the mill to the bar, and undoubtedly had some kind of meal there, washed down by beer after beer while he brooded on life's injustices.

It gave Margaret some hours of peace when he didn't come home for supper, but it was a peace dearly bought and paid for. Alcohol brought out the worst in Frank's nature, which, even at its best, fell far short of what a woman would want in a husband.

Margaret sighed. There was no point in thinking about it anymore. After thirty years of marriage, she knew what Frank was and what she could expect from him. Imagining what might have been would be more destructive to her sanity than any action of his.

There was a sharp creak from the staircase—near the bottom, she judged—as Frank slowly came upstairs, one hand tightly gripping the rail. It groaned in protest, and not for the first time, Margaret wondered what would happen if, just as Frank put his full weight on the railing, it pulled free from its support, leaving him with no secure handhold.

He would fall, she thought, but then he would just get up again, coming back up those stairs even angrier than before. He wouldn't die. He was too big, too strong, too angry to die. He would live forever, tying her to this house with him.

The steps continued, Frank's work boots scratching the fine wood finish as he stumbled a bit. Tomorrow she would bring the lemon oil and a soft rag to remove all traces of Frank from the boards. It wouldn't be easy. Frank's marks were hard to hide.

As he came closer, Margaret willed her breathing to be light and shallow. Perhaps when he paused at her doorway, he would think her asleep, and go on to his room, to sleep off the effects of too much beer.

Sometimes that happened, although it was hard for Margaret to relax even once she heard his door shut, afraid he might yet change his mind and return for her.

And in the end, it didn't matter whether he came in or left her alone. Her peace of mind was shattered anyway.

The landing groaned as Frank put his weight on the loose board, and Margaret waited, the silence stretching like a fine cord around her throat, making it almost impossible to draw a breath.

"Margaret." His voice, harsh in the darkness, rasped along her spine like a file on metal. She let out her breath and waited in the darkness. "I told you not to leave the damn light on." The door opened, and in the darkness, Margaret could almost discern the darker shadow that was her husband. She took a deep breath, forcing it past the constriction in her throat.

"It's late, Frank," she said, hearing the pleading note in her voice and hating herself for it. "Why don't you go to bed? You'll be tired in the morning."

He moved closer to the bed, leaning one hand unsteadily on the wall.

PERIPHERAL VISIONS AND OTHER STORIES

"So what if it's late?" His voice slurred a bit, but lost none of its anger. "A man's entitled to a drink or two after working hard all day. But you don't care, do you?" moving closer to the bed. "All you care about is spending money—my money! I'm the one who has to go there each day—to the dirt, the heat, and those bastards that run the place!

"But you don't care," and now Margaret could smell the beer on his breath as his face came closer, looming out of the darkness like a storm cloud. "You'd like me gone all the time so you could spend my money any way you want! Answer me, damn you!" and he grasped her graying hair in one meaty fist, jerking her upright on the lumpy mattress.

It was like all the other times, and while Margaret's body struggled to free itself from his angry hold, her mind soared away from the present—from the fingers that pulled and probed and pinched, from the mouth that hurt her with words as harsh as any blows.

She focused on the next day, the next week, the next month. It was a trick she had learned from bitter experience, and it had stood her in good stead many times before. But now, it was getting harder to shut out the painful present. She was growing old, after all.

She would wash windows, she decided, and starch the white curtains hanging in the living room. Perhaps if she mended the weak spots, they would last another year. Clean windows would let in the spring sunshine, giving the house the illusion of warmth and light. If only Frank would let her plant some flowers. Just a few—impatiens or petunias or begonias. Just something beautiful and alive to brighten up the yard.

Maybe by the back steps, she thought, her head dodging another blow almost automatically. Surely he couldn't object to a tiny square of flowers. Anyway, he went out back so rarely it might be weeks before he even knew they were there.

Her mind caught the picture she envisioned, imagining the softness of the petals, the delicate scent of flowers blooming in the sunlight. It was the way she once dreamed about the child she never had.

And by the time Frank left the room, she had convinced herself a few plants could be bought and set in the soil without arousing his anger.

Impatiens, she decided, absently wiping away a trickle of blood from the corner of her mouth. Tiny delicate impatiens, pink and white and bright red.

The next morning, after Frank left for work, Margaret sat on the back steps, the healing warmth of the early morning sunshine easing her aching muscles. She looked at the weedy patch to the side of the steps, and imagined it blossoming in the summer. Maybe when Frank saw it, he wouldn't mind. Maybe....

She walked down the steps, slowly because her side hurt where Frank had punched her, and knelt down in the grass. She pulled a few weeds and then scooped the soft dirt in her hand, letting it fall back onto the ground like a fine black rain. It was good rich soil. The plants would do well there. She pulled a few more weeds and then, intoxicated by the sight of the cleared space, continued working, ignoring the pain in her ribs and the stiffness in her shoulders. By lunchtime, the patch was waiting for her flowers, and Margaret was in a fever of impatience, because she couldn't go out and buy them right away.

Not with those bruises on her arm or the swollen lip, all red and sore. Someone was bound to ask awkward questions or give her the kind of look she had encountered before—pity and contempt all mixed together. She didn't care what they thought, she told herself time and time again. But she hated those looks all the same.

They had no right to pass judgment. They didn't understand—not about Frank or how his temper drove him to lose control. They didn't understand about Margaret either, and how, at her age, the prospect of starting over with no skills, no experience, was more frightening than any torture Frank could devise.

She just wished that sometime life would go more smoothly, so Frank wouldn't be so angry and she wouldn't have to spend long evenings shrinking at the sound of his key in the lock and his heavy tread upon the stairs.

The rest of the afternoon Margaret spent washing windows and ironing curtains as she had planned the night before. But while her hands were busy with those tasks, her mind wandered out to the cleared patch of ground, seeing again the fine black dirt, imagining the roots of the new plants running though the soil in search of food and water.

It had been years since Margaret had allowed herself to care about another living thing, and the urge was all the stronger for having been denied.

It was midnight before Frank came home, stumbling into the house and bumping into walls. He must have drunk more than usual, Margaret thought, as she heard him fall on the steps. Reluctantly, she left her bed to help him climb the rest of the stairs. But it was hard going. Frank leaned heavily on her shoulder, his breath coming in short hard gasps as he gripped the stair rail for support.

Margaret heard it groan with strain, and fearing it wouldn't be able to take it all, she tried to shift more of her husband's weight onto her shoulders.

"Damn it, leave me alone," he muttered, while grasping her shoulder in a bruising grip. "I can do it myself." He stumbled a few more steps, dragging her along with him. Margaret lost her balance, falling painfully to her knees.

"Frank, stop! I can't get back up with you leaning on me!" she cried, but he didn't answer. Instead, he pulled her along a few more steps before releasing her to finish his climb, now hanging with both hands to the wooden pole.

Margaret watched him, rubbing her arm where he had gripped it so tightly.

It was too much, she thought dully. I shouldn't have to live like this.

The next morning, she noticed the scrape marks along the wall, and the way the stair rail quivered in her hand. It should be tightened, maybe even reinforced, she thought. Maybe once she planted the flowers (her mind was never very far from the flowerbed) she would take the screwdriver and tighten the brass supports.

The flowerbed—she could hardly wait until Frank left for work. Today was the day she would buy her flowers. Her bruises had gone away—most of them, anyway. And she had saved some money from her grocery allowance to buy the few plants she needed.

And later, setting the tiny plants in their new homes, she marveled at their beauty and delicacy. The colors—red and white and pink, just as she had planned—shone like jewels against the velvet soil. How could anyone object to a few flowers? They cost so little and were so beautiful.

Maybe he would stop at the bar tonight, she thought hopefully. Then, by the time he came home, it would be dark. It might be days before he saw the flowers. And when he did, he might be in a better mood. He might even let them stay—after he relieved his anger at her disobedience. But a few blows were a small price to pay for the precious bit of color and light in her life.

Late that night, long after Frank had fallen into a heavy sleep, a storm came up. And when Margaret opened the back door to check on her flowers, she could see the damage the rain had done.

"Oh, my poor flowers!" she cried, hurrying down the steps to brush away the dirt spattered on their blossoms and set the roots more firmly in the damp soil.

They have to be all right, she thought desperately. I don't have any more money.

Heedless of the time, she worked feverishly, finally reassured by the sight of the thin stems, once more upright in the bed.

"Where the hell are you?" Frank's bellows recalled her to the present, and she realized his coffee wasn't ready—that any moment he would come outside looking for her and her treasure would be exposed to his sight.

Scrambling to her feet, Margaret tried to enter the kitchen before Frank realized where she had been. But she was too late.

It was always too late, she thought.

He was there, filling the doorway with his great angry bulk, looking first at her, then past her to where the flowers were soaking up the first early rays of the sun.

"What in the hell is this?" he demanded, and he strode to the bed to kick at the dirt. "I told you no flowers!"

Her stomach tightened and she braced herself for the blows she was certain to come. But he turned back to the flowerbed.

"Frank, no!" she wailed as he crushed the life from the blossoms with his heavy work boots. They couldn't survive that kind of abuse, she thought, watching him as tears ran down her face. They weren't as strong as she was.

Later, she couldn't remember how many times Frank hit her or how long his tirade lasted. But when he finally left, she pulled herself to the back door and gazed, white-faced and grieving, at the broken dying flowers.

"My poor babies," she whispered. "How could he hurt you so?"

She just couldn't let him do that again. Somehow Frank would have to be kept from killing her flowers.

Later that night, she heard the sound of the front door lock, and then Frank's heavy unsteady tread as he started up the staircase. It took him several tries to find the narrow wooden stair rail, which groaned alarmingly as it took his weight—the sound echoing through the dark house. He was a heavy man, she knew. The stair rail was thin and the screws old and loose. It would take so little for the rail to break free.

And in the end, it didn't take much at all. Somewhere, near the top, the brass screws pulled free from the wall. The rail, robbed of its support, in turn robbed Frank of his.

It seemed forever before the echoes faded—the sound Frank's body made as it fell head over heels down the narrow staircase to land, in a heap, at the bottom.

Margaret lay quietly in her bed, waiting for Frank to rise and begin cursing. But there was no sound from the floor below—not for five minutes, then ten, then twenty.

And by the time the ambulance came, Margaret knew there would never be noise again.

"It came loose," she explained to the paramedics as she gestured toward the railing, now broken in two. "He had too much to drink," that much they could tell just by the smell of him, "and it pulled loose when he was coming upstairs."

An accident, she repeated to herself as she went back to bed after they had left, taking Frank with them. And now he was dead.

And holding onto that thought, she fell into a deep, dreamless sleep.

The next morning she awoke far past her usual time, but her first fears were calmed as she remembered the events of the last few hours. Stretching her muscles gently, she lay there for a moment, marveling at how different her room looked, with the morning sunshine slipping past the tree branches to shine directly into her room.

Finally she arose, pulling on her robe and absentmindedly patting the bulge in its pocket. There was so much to do, she thought as she straightened the rug at the foot of the staircase, now that Frank was gone.

First things first: taking a sheet of newspaper out to the pitiful remains of her flowerbed, she tenderly lifted the broken stems and torn roots from the dirt, laying them on the open sheet.

Gently, she arranged the plants as though readying a body for burial, finally folding the sides over and across before laying the small bundle on top of the trash can.

"I'll have to buy new flowers," she said aloud, stretching in the sunlight before going back into the kitchen.

Then, she took the screwdriver from the pocket of her robe and put it back into the drawer where she always kept it. She'd have to make sure she fixed the rail as well, as soon as she came back from the store.

Standing in the kitchen doorway, she gazed up at the blue sky, free of clouds and warm with sunlight.

"I'll go shopping right after breakfast," she decided. "It's a good day for planting."

PERIPHERAL VISIONS AND OTHER STORIES

BURNING BRUSHES

"The brushes are burning."

My grandmother's murmur echoes in the room, flowing over neatly sharpened pencils and sheets of empty paper. When I was a child, I took her words literally and would peer around the doorway of the place she called her "studio," hoping to catch a glimpse of sparks or the scent of smoke in the air.

Instead, all I saw was a tiny woman, enveloped in her dead husband's work shirt, the filbert brush held tightly in her paint-stained hand.

Peering intently at the canvas before her, she would be oblivious to my presence, and once the bristles darted at the canvas, I would withdraw, knowing it would be hours before she would enter the world again.

Most of my grandmother's canvases are stacked in my spare bedroom. I was chosen to be the curator of her art as the only other family member with "creative tendencies"—said in the same tone of voice that would have been used had I inherited some strange familial disease. While other family members fought over silver and china, old draperies and bedding, I alone requested and was granted the canvas and paints.

I thought they would inspire me. Instead, they served as a reproach, mocking my inability to produce anything more than the occasional piece of writing that would find a home in newsprint-grade magazines.

My grandmother was twenty-three when she started painting, and she kept on painting even after she buried my grandfather and sold the home in which they had lived for over forty years. She moved into my mother's house when I was in my mid-twenties and expecting my first child and was still there when my daughter graduated from high school. By then, however, her arthritic fingers could no longer grasp the brushes, and her eyes could no longer distinguish between the white of the canvas and the soft yellows and greens that characterized her work. But she would still disappear into the studio each morning, perhaps hoping for some residual warmth from brushes that no longer flamed with life.

I am twenty years older than my grandmother was when she released the fire within her, and theoretically have more time to pursue my writing. My day job hardly taxes my creative abilities. Monitoring cash flow and receivables is left-brain occupation. And once I return home, there are no crying children or mounds of dirty laundry to demand my attention. Nothing, in short, to keep me from the lined tablet and pencils, the keyboard and reams of twenty-pound bond.

Yet, aside from a few insignificant pieces, I have been unable to write. *My* brushes no longer burn—and, if they ever did, the ashes are so cold that it would take more fuel than I possess to start the fire again. Some nights, I toy with the idea of quitting my job, taking what little savings I had managed to amass after my divorce, and writing full time every day.

Or maybe, I think, I should cut myself off from my family—tell my parents to stop calling with their endless complaints about each other, explain to my daughter that she is old enough to solve her problems on her own. Perhaps isolation is the key—and yet, my grandmother painted in a houseful of people.

It would be so much easier to let it all go, to take the desire and pack it away, like maternity clothes that are no longer needed. And occasionally, I try to do it. I stack the papers in a carton, pile the unfinished manuscripts into a drawer, turn my desk back into the dining room table. The books on writing are given away, and subscriptions to literary magazines are not renewed.

I consider taking courses in real estate or trips to foreign lands. I make plans with old friends for dinner and agree to meet relative strangers for drinks. Houseplants are purchased, apartment walls re-papered, make-up and hairstyle updated.

But some part of me knows these to be futile acts. And when I least expect it, the urge returns. Like a junkie, I scrabble frantically through the closet, searching for that half-finished novel or essay, certain that the ideas, so long awaited, are now ready to be fully developed on paper.

I brush aside the latest movie review, and set the paper-clipped pages before me, pencil at the ready, fingers itching to write the rest of the story. Then quickly, like the brief flame from a match, the fire dies. And unlike the ashes my grandmother could breathe to life again and again, I am left with nothing—no spark, no warmth. The pages remain empty, the pencil point as sharp as when I took it from its resting place. And I am cold—so cold that all the fires of hell would not be able to warm me.

"I cannot *write*," I tell my mother when I call her late Friday night, but she doesn't hear me. Or perhaps she does, but is unable to offer any words of comfort, at a loss to understand this strange need that drove her mother and now her child.

"I *cannot* write," I tell my daughter the following morning, but she is caught up with the demands of a new baby and unable to sympathize with someone she believes is only undergoing a "mid-life crisis."

"*I* cannot write!" But there is no one in the empty room to reassure me, console me or tell me that this will change and someday I will be able to put into words everything that exists only in my mind. So I push aside the desire, hoping it will dry up like the paints in the tubes and stop tormenting me.

And for a while it does, until the day comes when I can no longer ignore inspiration's siren call. With no one left to talk to, I turn to my grandmother, long dead but still living in those canvases that hold her more firmly than any wooden casket ever could. That afternoon, I take her paintings one by one and arrange them around the room, balancing some against the couch and leaning others on the windowsills. Running out of space, I begin to hang them on the empty walls, driving nails into the plaster, not stopping until I feel the wooden studs catch the steel.

I spend the rest of the weekend displaying my grandmother's work in my small apartment, turning what was once a bare set of rooms into a gallery commemorating her life.

By Sunday midnight, my rooms are bathed in emerald and lime, topaz and lemon—all the ranges and hues of yellow and green that marked my grandmother's work. I walk from one painting to another as though attending a private showing, examining the pictures intently. Perhaps there was a key, perhaps somewhere under the layers of pigment was the secret my grandmother knew, but waited too long to tell me.

But the secret, if indeed it exists, remains concealed. All I see are shadows and outlines, barely visible under the colors. A child's silhouette here, an open window there, a vacant rocking chair in one painting while in another a coat lies carelessly on the floor.

Worn out by longing, I drag my pillows from my bed and lie down in the middle of the floor, surrounded by the colors of warmth and life. And when the alarm clock rings several hours later, I am startled awake, torn from a dream only vaguely remembered. The morning light streams into the room, and the paintings come alive, bursting anew with energy.

I should be dressing for work. I should be drinking my morning coffee while carefully applying make-up to hide the shadows from the late night. Instead, I circle the room again, the paintings calling out to me, the still-hidden secret tantalizingly out of reach.

Until I reach the last painting—her first, her initials and the date carefully traced in burnt umber at the bottom right-hand corner. A small painting compared to the others, it was simply done on a canvas barely two-foot square.

It is a painting *of* a painting—an artist's easel carefully depicted, leaning against a half-opened cedar chest. When I had viewed the painting before, my eyes focused on the picture on the canvas—nothing more than an old-fashioned stone bridge, crossing a stream. I wondered at the time at my grandmother's choice. It seemed so basic, so amateur—the kind of drawing-within-a-drawing art teachers give as assignments to beginning students.

But now for the first time, I notice the chest against which the canvas is placed. There is material spilling from the inside. I recognize the lace shawl that was part of my grandmother's trousseau, and the baby quilt she had carefully sewn in preparation for my mother's birth. Remnants of her past life, carefully packed away in a chest now serving as a support for the new existence she was creating.

And for the first time I understand that my grandmother did not seek to discard her old life, but to incorporate it into her work, one feeding the other to keep the flame alive. If there was a secret, if there was indeed some magic in how she kept the fire burning, it lay in her ability to use the memories of the past to nurture her future.

Not distance but integration. Not separateness, but assimilation. Inspiration and desire—one feeding the other, ready to set my own brush on fire.

I pick up a pencil and begin to write.

PERIPHERAL VISIONS AND OTHER STORIES

MEMORIES OF MUSIC

"My wife was a wonderful baker. Each Saturday, she would bake four loaves of bread, and then, before the oven cooled, put in some pizzas, round as harvest moons. We had an outside oven, and before I left for work—we worked Saturdays back then and were glad of the labor—it was my job to split enough wood to fill the oven.

"And when I came home at lunch—I could easily walk the few miles from the mill to the house—she would be at the oven, pulling bread out, sliding bread in, her movements so rhythmic you would think she heard music."

He remembered how the sweat would trickle its way down her face and a few strands of her hair would free themselves from the twisted coil at the nape of her neck to curl around her face. Sometimes, when he kissed her, he could taste the salt on her flushed cheek.

"That will be $3.10," the cashier announced in a bored voice, and the old man regretfully pulled the money from his creased wallet. Nowadays, two loaves of bread cost what he made in a week's hard labor long ago.

"I wouldn't mind," he said, handing over the money, "if it tasted as good as what my wife made. But it doesn't. It tastes like sawdust." He looked at the people in the line behind him, to see if anyone agreed. "Sawdust mixed with air."

But they just shifted their tired feet and said nothing. Maybe, he thought, they were afraid he would stay there rambling on about days gone by and delaying them from their busy lives.

But he wasn't like that, he thought to himself. That was what other old people did—lonely old men and women who had no one to talk to. He had seen them in the park, stopping every passerby they could, telling them what was wrong with the world. And he had seen the look in their eyes—lonely and afraid, as if they needed to hear their own voice to know they were alive.

He lifted the paper bag of groceries with a sigh and walked toward the exit, pausing long enough to make certain the electric door would open and stay open. Electric doors brought an end to small courtesies, like holding a door for a lady, since the door opened and shut on its own accord.

Years ago, women were considered delicate creatures, and it fell to men to protect them. Yet it was the women who bore children, one after the other, swelling like rosebuds coming to bloom. A man could plant the seed, but it took the woman's power to bring it to life in that fertile, hidden darkness. And it took a woman's strength to force that life out into the daylight.

He shifted the bag to his other arm as he stopped at the newsstand to buy the afternoon paper, even though the headlines were always the same—rape, murder, beatings.

"Never good news," he said, shaking his head as he handed over his payment to the man behind the counter. "It wasn't like that years ago, you know. People were better back then."

But there was still death, he had to admit. Death from wars, death from sickness.

Each year, the spring thaw would bring runny noses and sore throats to the children that mothers doctored with remedies from the old country. Fevers burned the tender faces bright red, and then died away, and the children grew well again.

Most children—but not all. Sometimes, the sickness burrowed deep into the young bodies, finding the weak spots. Sometimes, when the fever died, it left not the coolness of health but the coldness of death.

When her fever burned the fiercest, their daughter had alternately clung to his wife's hand and then pushed her away, crying at terrifying visions only she could see. Her small body was speckled with red dots, and the dampness from the cool cloths evaporated against her hot flesh. The sickroom had a smell to it, a brassy odor that clung to the bed sheets.

The fever faded but left behind a child with eyes dark against a pale face and skin that no longer blushed with life but was white as marble. And two parents, unable to do anything more than wait for the outcome.

Sometimes, his wife would lean her head against his chest, too tired even to wrap her arms around him. He saw the circles deepen under her eyes, the skin stretch tighter across her face from lack of eating, and he didn't know what he should do, what he *could* do but send silent prayers to a merciful God.

Each day, he would rise in the chill light of dawn, stopping for a moment in the sickroom, and then went to work where, when pieces broke, he knew how to put them back together again. Each evening, he would sit with the child, so his wife could sleep before it was her turn to come back to the sickroom. Often, he remembered, she would choose to stay by the bedside, sitting on the floor and resting her head on the bed.

That's how he found her one morning, with their daughter's cold hand clasped in hers. And she had never forgiven herself for falling asleep while their child drifted away.

"It's a hard world," the newsstand vendor agreed, and for a moment, the old man was startled. He had forgotten that he wasn't alone. "But what can you do? That's the price of progress."

"But what kind of progress brings so much misery?" Not waiting for an answer, he tucked the paper under his arm and continued down the street to the small park near his house. Sometimes, if the weather was warm, he would sit on the bench and read through the news, carefully folding back each page.

In the background would be the music of the children, as balls were tossed and bats were swung, as races were run by the swiftest while the rest cheered. He didn't mind the noise. Since his wife died, the silence at home was almost deafening. He would read his paper and drink in the welcome sounds of children playing until it was time to go home.

Today there were only two people in the park, a young girl on a swing and her mother, resting on the bench where he usually sat. With a small bow, he asked, "May I sit down?" and disarmed by his courtesy, she gestured toward the seat in welcome.

In silence, they watched the child as her fat legs pumped the swing higher. Then, as it began the inevitable downward arc, she leaned back, letting her braids dangle until, at the lowest point, they brushed the ground below her feet. The breeze blew her bangs from her forehead and billowed her open jacket behind her like a sail.

"All children like the swings," he observed then, and the woman nodded her head in agreement.

"Until they grow old enough for video games," she added with a laugh. "So much for the simple pleasures of youth."

"Years ago, children did not have many toys," the old man said. "A ball and bat, and a doll for the girls. And marbles. Do children play with marbles any more, I wonder? But there was always work for them to do—help in the house or out in the garden. Children had to help out. There was too much work and too little time. Everyone had to work. Even the young ones could be taught to pull weeds or pinch bugs from growing plants."

The woman nodded again, her eyes on the child as she swung back and forth.

"It's different now," she said finally. "No one has the time or space for a garden. Parents have to work, to pay the bills and buy the food."

"And the food is not even as good," the old man answered. "When the tomatoes were ripe, my wife would pick them, still warm from the sun, and the juice would nearly be bursting from the skin. She would scald them, peel off the skins, and then quickly dice them into a pot-with bits of garlic and chunks of onion. The house was filled with the smell of the sauce she was making, and if you breathed deeply enough, you could taste the tomato in the air."

The woman listened with an air of interest, although her eyes never left the swing. But he was encouraged to continue.

"She baked—how my wife baked! Fruit pies—the crust so delicate and flaky you could give it to a baby. At Christmas time, every surface held racks of cooling pastries and fruit braids, decorated cookies and flat pans of boiled candies like sheets of stained glass. And always singing to herself, Christmas carols from the old country."

"She must have been a wonderful woman," the woman said but he hardly heard her, so caught was he by the pictures of the past.

"On Sunday," the words spilling from him now, a tide from the ocean of memory, "she would stuff a fat chicken with cubes from bread she had baked earlier and dried. She raised the chickens from little peeps in a small pen I had made for her. When they were old enough, she would pick one out and, with a cleaver almost too heavy for her to handle, she would chop off the head.

"I'm sorry," he added, as the woman frowned, "but that was how it was done. No neatly wrapped packages of parts in the store. It was all done, start to finish, birth to death, in the home."

"It must be lonely for you," she finally said, with a sidelong glance at the old man. "All those years together and now…" She let her words trail off into the stillness.

"And now," he answered after a moment, "now there is no music, no dancing." At her puzzled look, he explained, "Just an expression. My wife and I, we didn't dance much. There was too much work to do to have time for dancing."

At their wedding, though, they had danced—all the lively country dances until, hearts racing and faces flushed, they had slowed for the last dance of all. And he had clasped her in his arms and felt her pulse racing and wasn't sure if it was from the exertion or his closeness.

In the distance, the sound of the church bells could be heard, chiming the hour and his companion quickly got to her feet.

"I must go now. I'm afraid *I'm* one of those mothers who buys her food instead of growing it. And I'd better get to the store if I'm to cook dinner tonight. Perhaps we'll see you here again."

"Perhaps," he agreed, and watched the two of them leave, the mother's quick step matched by the daughter's running feet. Then he leaned back, letting the sun warm his face. It did not seem possible, on sunny days like this, that his wife would not be waiting at home for him.

He remembered when they met. He had been keeping company with another girl, but something in his wife's dark eyes, the way she tossed her hair, spelled doom for the other romance, and he courted her with all the controlled passion a young man might show.

On their wedding night, she had cried with love, and then clung to him, as though she feared he might leave. She never knew he was hopelessly, helplessly, bound to her with ties of passion and love he could barely comprehend.

He couldn't let her see his weakness. He was a man and had to be strong, the sturdy oak under which she could seek shelter. He did not know, until she was gone, how much of his strength came from her presence, how much grace and music she had brought to his life.

But at the end, the music played for her alone. He had brushed her white hair back from her face and held her closely. She smiled at him then, the ghost of a young girl still in her eyes, but the music was stronger and little by little, she had danced away.

Once she had gone, the music stopped, leaving behind just a memory of what had been. Only by talking of her could he bring back the faint melody that was their life.

He pushed himself up from the bench and walked slowly toward home. There he met the postman, who handed him the day's mail, saying, "Nice day today."

"Yes, a nice day," the old man agreed. "You know, on a day like today, my wife would be hanging clothes on the line, snapping the sheets until the creases were gone. My wife was a hard worker. And what a baker—have I told you how wonderful a baker she was? And always singing..."

And just for a moment, he could hear her voice, sweet and sure, in the distance.

AFTER THE STORM

The late-afternoon light was yellow, not the clear gold of sunshine but a jaundiced shade that reminded Sara of illness and hospital rooms, hanging over the lawn and trees like a piece of cellophane.

The air, heavy with heat and humidity, pressed against her chest and her muscles strained with each inhalation. All around her, there was an ominous stillness, an absolute cessation of sound and movement as if the world were holding its breath in fear of what might be coming.

Backlit, the storm clouds massed far in the sky—a council of war planning the next battle—and Sara crinkled her eyes against the sickly light as it grew brighter and more painful. Tales of Kansas twisters and Florida hurricanes tormented her mind, and she found herself hurrying through the small house, checking windows and closing doors, all the while nervously glancing outdoors to gauge the proximity of the storm.

But really, what good did it do to watch the slow but inevitable procession of clouds, menacing and black-browed? She couldn't stop them. There was nothing she could do but wait for the storm and all its attendant warriors: the lightning bolts, the roaring thunder, the powerful gusts of water and wind that would bend and break her if she dared go outdoors.

Even inside there was precious little protection. Lightning could strike at the wires joining her house to the tall pole outside and, in one blinding burst, deprive her of power and light. She would be lost in the darkness, unable to find her way out.

Or water, cascading like Niagara Falls down the eaves, could find a weakness in the roof—the slightest hint of vulnerability between one shingle and the next—and like a guerrilla warrior, slip into the attic and then the house proper, while she could do no more than helplessly watch its approach.

Sara's house was solidly built of oak and brick, and she had once thought it to be impervious to attacks. Now she knew the truth. Nothing was safe. Anything could be threatened. There were so many unprotected places in a house, in a body, in a life. There were so many ways for the storm to enter. And when it happened, where was one to go?

Thunder rattled the windows, sending shock waves coursing through her. "I will not be afraid," she said aloud, her trembling voice barely heard over the sound of the storm. "It's only noise. It can't hurt me."

But still she shivered as the storm drew nearer, the reverberations of thunder shaking the house until the chandelier danced on its narrow gold chain.

If she was brave enough to approach the window (but, she reminded herself, one should never look out the window during a storm), she might see it on the horizon—a vague, shapeless, hulking mass, hungry for whatever it could find and frighten. But courage had dried up in her, as the ground outside had dried in the relentless heat. There was nothing left inside.

The screen door slammed against its frame, and Sara rushed to catch it, her thin fingers fumbling with the catch. A heavier bolt, a stronger lock? But what good were locks and bolts when you didn't know from which direction the storm was coming, what would be its next target?

Shutting the heavy wooden front door, she retreated into the living room, taking shelter in the old overstuffed easy chair and pulling a blanket around her. Despite the heat, her body was cold, fear dancing up and down the vertebral staircase of her delicate spine.

The storm was coming. There was no further action she could take to protect herself.

Eyes shut, she trembled as the earth shook with the force of the thunder. The lightning found her where she hid and pierced her thin eyelids with sword-points of light until she was unable to see clearly when she dared open her eyes.

And still it stormed. A gust of wind swirled like a mad thing through the yard, carrying bits of leaves and twigs in its grasp. Trees bent half-double, begging for mercy though none was forthcoming, and the air, so humid a few moments ago, was now past cool to cold.

Suddenly, the clouds were directly overhead—a low ceiling almost touching the roofline. Lightning danced and darted around the house like a possessed creature seeking entrance, as the thunder vibrated through every bit of wood, every tiny ornament on the bookshelf, every nerve of her thin, defenseless body.

And then, more quickly than it had come, the storm died down. Weakened by its own fury, nearly lifeless, its lifeblood poured out in clear rivers over the thirsty ground, the storm had nowhere to go but into non-existence. Lacking the power to survive its own intensity, it slowly dissipated, with just a few lingering flashes, a few half-hearted rumblings.

Sara slipped from the rocker, stiff-legged and chilled, and tentatively pushed open the casement windows. Damp, fresh air washed over her, cleansing away the sweat from her face. As she watched, a few brave sparrows, hunting for worms who in turn were hunting for life-giving moisture, hopped from the shelter of the trees to land lightly on the wet blades of grass.

How did they manage to survive the wind and rain? she wondered, marveling at their resilience. Was it courage or just luck—and did it really matter as long as the outcome was the same?

Hesitatingly, she ran her fingers down her rib cage and across the thin scar, now nearly healed. Better than average odds, the doctor had told her. With treatment—and luck—she could very well be one of those who went on to grow strong and healthy. For the first time in weeks, she allowed herself to believe their words, to hope for a future.

Opening the front door, she walked outside, stepping gently into the puddles and shivering as the cold water lapped over her toes. It was too late in the day for the sun to warm and ultimately evaporate the pools.

Instead, through the long night, they would reflect twinkling points of hope to illuminate the darkness.

GOING HOME

"Can you tell me please which way to Union Station?"

No one answered her, no one stopped to point out the streets to take, the buses to board. They looked right through her—she didn't exist, not for them.

Sara should have been used to it. Two years on the streets of LA had provided her with an education she had not expected, and the first lesson was: you are invisible. Unfortunately, however, she was never invisible to her mother. *She* could see everything—except she never saw Sara leaving, although the signs were there, like itineraries scattered around the room. The drinking, the drugs—what else were they but a form of escape?

From what, Sara didn't really know. And although she did get away, the need for escape wasn't really satisfied—not in a new place, not in this new life.

"Get out of the way!" and Sara was pushed roughly into the corner of a building. She rubbed her shoulder, the lightweight jacket providing little padding from the sharp stonework, and then kept walking.

When she first came to the City of Angels, the land of sunshine and opportunity (or so she had thought), she brought with her the quick retorts that she had used so effectively back East. She had pictured herself as the edgy tough punk girl who wouldn't take any shit from anyone.

But LA wasn't like home. Drugs, yes, but not the same. Even the sunlight was a sham. She never felt warm, not even once. LA streets were just as hard and cold as those in New York.

"Union Station—look, just tell me which way to go!"

Sara heard the desperation in her voice. That frightened her, more than the faces of the people who walked past her, not seeing her, not hearing her. She *should* know the way—she had been here long enough to learn how to navigate through the streets. But her brain just wasn't functioning right.

Foggy, tired—that was it, she was tired. It had been a late night last night (where did she sleep, anyway?) and maybe some bad stuff too, although now she couldn't even remember what she had taken. Couldn't have been anything too good—she didn't have much money. Turning tricks didn't pay as well as she had thought it would. Or was it just her? Maybe she just didn't appeal to them: those button-down suit guys who took cabs from Figueroa or Spring in the Financial District, those plastic-faced, would-be actors smiling, always smiling, just in case someone somewhere was looking for a face, those hard-edged agents who tooktooktook but gave so little in return.

People said New York was cold. But LA was colder—the appearance of warmth was just a fake. It was cold like dry ice, burning when she touched it. And she had the scars to prove it.

Sara rubbed her arm where the knife wound was slowly healing, although the edges of the cut were still flaming red. She should have gone to the clinic. They at least would have given her a shot and stitched her up before sending her to the cops as a vagrant. But one stay within those walls had been enough. Never again.

The sun was bright—too bright—and her head was aching. It was so warm today, unusual for February. In southern

PERIPHERAL VISIONS AND OTHER STORIES

California, January and February were months of gray skies and drizzling rain, not this heat that seemed to rise from the sidewalks to engulf her. Her throat hurt, too, and she would kill for a glass of cold water. Or ice cream, like the ice cream her mother used to get her when they went to the park. There was a guy there selling Parker's Frozen Custard, she remembered, and he always topped her cone with a cherry piece before handing it to her.

Sundays—they would go there on Sundays in the summer after church. When did they stop going? When she was ten? Twelve? Fourteen? After her mother had found her stash of cigarettes? Smelled the beer on her breath? Noticed her pupils, dilated like great black holes into which both of them were falling in slow motion?

Sara sank down on the bench, not caring about the debris that stuck to its surface. After you have slept on the streets enough times, you didn't stop to examine anything too closely before using it: benches, bottles, needles, people.

Her mother was a clean freak, she remembered. Everything had to be spotless, sanitized, safe. But nothing ever was safe—Sara knew that long before her mother did—people least of all. Not the guy who swore he loved you and would always love you if only you did what he wanted. Not the teacher who said he wanted to help you but only really wanted to touch you. Not the last guy her mother had been dating before Sara left, who said he wanted to be like a dad to Sara, but had something else in mind.

Although Mike—now he wasn't too bad. He had, at least, given her food and cleaned her up and bought her some clothes before he asked for anything. And really, was it so much that he asked for? After all, rooms—even dives like the one on

Success Avenue (and what a joke *that* name was since the Willowbrook neighborhood was high on the crime list) cost a lot. It was only fair that she had to pay her way to stay there, just like the rest of the women. And it wasn't like she could get a real job. Who would hire her?

Cleaned up, she didn't look so bad. The waif-like look was a big draw for a certain type. After months in the city, she had lost so much weight that her eyes and cheekbones were all they saw. That and her body, unmistakably a woman's even if it was almost skeletal. But they never saw *her*—the real her, Sara herself.

But that was okay. She didn't see them either.

So she did her bit and really it wasn't so bad. And Mike fed her and gave her some money to spend as she liked from what she earned. Sometimes, she would make a joke—ask for her "allowance"—but after a while the word hurt when she spoke it. It smacked too much of being a child, which reminded her of being home. And she couldn't go there—not in her mind and certainly not for real.

Not after everything. Although when she made that last call—two years ago, was it?—her mother sounded like she wanted to talk with her. Maybe she might have even sent her some money. No—don't go there. It wouldn't have happened. Her mother would have told her what a fuck-up she was and how she had hurt her, and Sara couldn't have taken it. Not then.

She pulled herself up from the bench and started walking again. Maybe she would see someone she knew who could tell her which way to go. That's all she needed—nothing else, no money, no help. The last john—he had given her some extra money—"a bonus to make you smile" he had said—that she squirreled away to get her partway to where she was going.

PERIPHERAL VISIONS AND OTHER STORIES

That's all turning tricks was, really—a means to an end. A job. Something you do every day like being a stockbroker or accountant or nurse or teacher—just a job.

No big deal.

At least, it wasn't so hot anymore. Actually, it felt kind of chilly, and Sara pulled the jacket closer around her, buttoning the few buttons that remained. She hated being cold. It made her bones and skin hurt. On her bed, she had had a quilt her mother had made when she was pregnant with her. All during those nine months, her mother had stitched the pieces together. "I couldn't stitch up what happened between your dad and me, but I could at least stitch these pieces," she had told Sara once, during a moment when they had connected—really connected.

What had prompted that unusual state of affairs? Sara thought back, her forehead wrinkling with the effort of traversing the memories that crowded her brain. Must have been when her Grandma died—her mother had gotten the call after the fact, too late to go there and say—say what?

"I just wanted to tell her goodbye," she sobbed when Sara had come home from school to find her mother, huddled on the couch, still holding the phone. "I just wanted—" but she couldn't finish what she wanted. Maybe she didn't know herself what she wanted from the woman she barely spoke to from one month to the next.

The quilt—it was purple. No, violet—violet with cream edges. Every piece had some kind of violet color: a flower, a band, a pattern. Violet was the color of her birthstone—she had been born in the cold, dark month of February—and when she had turned ten, her mother had even repainted her bedroom walls a soft lavender.

When she left, Sara thought about taking the quilt but it was so big, so heavy and she was going to go to LA after all where it was hot and she wouldn't need it. So she left it for her mother to find, complete with the burn holes from the cigarettes she had smoked in bed. Her mother knew she smoked, told her to stop smoking, lectured and threatened her with warnings of cancer and fire and all manner of personal damage. But Sara had screamed at her to screw off, that she would do what she wanted.

And she did: liquor, drugs, sex. Told herself it was her choice, her right. Told herself she wanted to do it, had to do it. But somehow, once she was out of that place—"You're trying to make this a goddam prison!" she had screamed during one of their last fights—it wasn't as good as she thought it would be.

But then, what was?

Up ahead, she saw the sand-colored bell tower of the station. She was close, so close. She'd buy a ticket to Chicago and then take another train to Penn Station. And then—but she didn't want to think any farther than New York. She didn't know what would happen when she got back home, but it didn't matter. What mattered was that she was going home—whatever home was or would be.

Maybe the station would be warmer, and Sara walked a little faster, even though her legs were tired, even though she tripped on invisible cracks in the sidewalk. She had almost enough for a ticket. She only had to do it again and she'd have enough for the ticket and a burger. Or soup—chicken soup—homemade noodles. That's what her mom had made her when she was getting better from pneumonia that year.

She almost died—at least that's what she heard her mother tell her grandmother when she thought she was sleeping.

"I'm so scared," Sara heard her mother whisper into the hospital phone. "They keep giving her antibiotics and doing breathing treatments, but she can't breathe and just keeps coughing and, oh God, Mom, I think she might die!"

But she didn't, and after she was better—after she had swallowed gallons of chicken soup and felt good enough to get up and play and then go back to school, things went back to the way they had been (or the way they were going). And the fear in her mother's voice was gradually replaced with exasperation and then anger.

And Sara never even thought about that time, or how her mother must have felt, alone in that hospital room day after day, night after night—alone because her own mother wouldn't come to watch with her because they were fighting again, and even the phone call didn't move that cold, hard old woman from her place of righteousness.

Maybe she'd sit just for a minute on one of the benches outside the entrance, long enough to let the sun warm her. She was cold, really cold, and a bit dizzy. Maybe she was hungry. When did she eat last? *What* did she eat last?

Sara slumped down, leaning her head against the back of the bench. The sunlight danced across her face—her skin blotchy and pale even in California—and the strands of her lank, brown hair that had escaped the rubber band at the nape of her neck.

She would sit here for just a minute, maybe two. Just long enough to get warm. She was so cold. Then she would get up, pull herself together, buy the ticket for home. Home. Then maybe everything would be different.

PERIPHERAL VISIONS AND OTHER STORIES

ACCIDENTS WILL HAPPEN

The morning papers were full of the story: CYANIDE KILLER CLAIMS ANOTHER VICTIM! STOMACH REMEDY DEFINITE LINK!

Catherine carefully dumped the coffee grounds onto the center of the front page and then folded over the four corners, making a neat bundle. Robert didn't like to read the morning paper. He said it made him angry—all those stupid stories about people being robbed or killed or both—although Catherine sometimes privately wondered if Robert wouldn't be just as angry even without reading the news.

She carried the bundle of paper to the trash bin, wincing a bit when she raised the lid. Her shoulder was still sore, although the bruise had nearly faded. At least it wasn't her face this time. It was difficult to find make-up that would conceal scratches and bruise marks.

Catherine didn't read the paper very much herself. She didn't like the stories about violence—didn't approve of violence, especially when it led to someone's death.

Except maybe during a war, although it had been a war that had given Robert those "violent tendencies," as the psychiatrist's report had called his rages. But when she read the report, Catherine noticed the typist had left the "n" out of "violent." From that time on, she always pictured an angry Robert surrounded by purple clouds, as he himself turned a darker violet.

Now accidents, on the other hand—while Catherine didn't like the idea of anyone dying, accidents did seem the best way. No one to blame, just Lady Luck or Fate or the odds not being in your favor.

Sometimes people were sorry when someone else died, but other times, Catherine thought, the deaths must have seemed ordained by Providence as the perfect solution to an impossible situation.

These poisoning stories—Catherine wasn't sure if they fell under the murder or accident heading. Sometimes it was blamed on a mechanical malfunction or failure in the Quality Control Department. But other times it was a deliberate attempt to murder total strangers, with the chances of death evenly distributed between the lucky and unlucky consumers of the product.

How many people would this latest crime claim? Catherine wondered. How many would awaken with a hangover and take a dose of medicine and never have a hangover again? How many would fail to read the article in the morning newspaper before opening the bottle and ingesting the fatal dose?

Catherine herself had been very careful, not wanting any accidents to happen in her home. She had marked down the lot number on the list she kept hanging inside the kitchen cabinet door, and then had checked the stock in their medicine cabinet. The antacid was there—its lot number matching the one in the paper—and she had brought it downstairs.

She did this every time. Like the time the aspirins were found to be laced with strychnine—that was Lot Number 4300. Or the name-brand coffee holding bits of ground glass—Lot 66441.

And the can of mushroom soup with a touch of acid—poor mushrooms, Catherine thought at the time as she added the information to the ever-growing list. They were always being blamed for something.

Noises upstairs told her Robert had awakened. Soon he would be downstairs, demanding his breakfast and finding fault with everything she did.

The coffee would be too cold or the toast too brown—all just a prelude to another round of pinching and poking until he had to catch the morning train, leaving her to soak the worst of the bruises in ice water.

Sometimes that helped. But sometimes nothing helped.

There were heavy steps on the kitchen floor, and Catherine knew by the shrinking of her skin that Robert had come downstairs. She turned to face him, carefully closing the cabinet door.

"I have an awful headache," he muttered, pushing her out of the way as he reached for a glass.

Catherine trembled. She knew that the headache was a sign that last night had not been enough to dispel the purple clouds, and unconsciously she raised a hand to rub her shoulder.

Robert swallowed the water, then grabbed her painfully by the arm.

"Where's breakfast?" he demanded and shoved her again, harder. She caught her breath as her shoulder hit the wall. "How many times have I said to have the coffee ready when I come down?"

Robert gave her a final push and sank onto the kitchen chair, cradling his aching head in his large hands. Catherine looked at his hands in fascination. They were so big, so powerful—it was so hard sometimes to slip free of their grasp.

"Oh, my head," Robert groaned, and then raised his head and glared at her. "Can't you do something for me? And you'll have to call my boss. Tell him I can't come in today. I'm too damned sick. I just want to stay home."

Home—all day. Catherine's mind registered the words as she moved automatically to start the coffee. And he was so angry. And there was nowhere for her to go, even if she would be brave enough to leave. She would have to come home eventually.

"Get me something for my stomach. It hurts like hell. And hurry up," he added, throwing the saltshaker at her. "I can't take any more."

The morning sunshine streamed through the window, and Catherine closed her eyes against the glare. There was too much light. She could see everything far too clearly.

Almost without thinking, she moved to the cabinet, reaching past the cans of mushrooms to grasp the antacid and aspirin.

"I'll take care of it, Robert," she said as she carefully closed the door.

PERIPHERAL VISIONS AND OTHER STORIES

STARTING TO SURFACE

She had forgotten how humid the pool area was. Coming from the chill of the locker room, the damp air hit her like a blanket, making it difficult to draw a breath. Carrie felt as though she was suffocating, and, for a moment, she almost ran back to the relative comfort of the hallway.

Don't be ridiculous, she told herself, and walked toward the water. Just because you haven't been here for six months—not since it happened, not since....

But there she stopped her thoughts. She wasn't here to think. She was here to swim, to exercise muscles, to get rid of the tension that stiffened her neck and made her head ache by nightfall.

At least, the scratches and bruises had healed.

"You were lucky, you know," the doctor in the emergency room had said as he examined her. "It could have been much worse."

Worse? Carrie knew what he meant, of course. He might have had a gun or a knife. There might have been others with him. She might have died. Yes, it could have been worse.

Not that it was over, not by a long shot. If they caught him, not that her description was much help, there would be the trial to endure.

"Can't you be a little clearer about your attacker?" the officer had asked. "Tall or short? Thin or fat? Could you glimpse his skin color? Did he have an accent?"

But she couldn't remember much, except that he smelled like stale beer and cigarettes. After all, he had come from behind, just as she was unlocking her car in the parking deck. Even now, she could remember the frozen second when she thought, "It can't be happening to me" just before he threw some sort of cloth over her head and face, muffling her screams, her breath, her thoughts.

Afterwards, her mind ran in circles, focusing on random bits and pieces. Anything rather than think about what happened.

"This was a new blouse," she remembered thinking, as her fingers found several tears in the material. "I look a mess," she had thought, and gathering up her purse where he had flung it, she pulled out a comb and tried to run it through her tangled hair before she called the police. Even after they arrived, she kept pulling at the knots until the pain penetrated her frozen brain and she started to cry.

She didn't stop, not for a long time. She cried all through the examination, through the questioning by police, and all the way home, while Jeff drove the car, his hands clenching the steering wheel until she expected it to break in two.

"Carrie, are you okay? Are you hurt?" he had asked when he first came to the hospital. He had stood by the bedside, almost as if he was afraid to come any closer, to touch her, to hug her. And in a way, she was glad. She didn't want to be held. Not then. Not yet.

It wasn't until later that the questions came: "Was he bigger than you? How much bigger? Did he have a weapon? Didn't you look around before you got to the car?"

All those questions he asked her and the unspoken one was the loudest: "Why didn't you fight him?" because, of course, she hadn't. She had been too frightened to react, respond. All Carrie had wanted was for it to be over, for him to go away. She was almost willing to pretend it never happened. If the other couple hadn't come along when they did and found her pulling hysterically at her hair while her skirt lay on the cement floor, she might have considered doing just that.

Anything rather than face what had happened. Because, after all, rape is what happens to other people. To young girls who are careless. To women who frequent bars on the bad side of town. Rape doesn't happen to thirty-two-year-old professional women who are at their place of business, who are *where* they should be *when* they should be, who dress conservatively and never speak to strangers.

That's what she used to think, anyway.

But she was here today to swim, not think. She walked around the pool deck to the shallow end, and slowly descended the metal ladder, shivering as the cold water climbed higher on her thighs.

She used to like to swim. She liked the whole camaraderie of coming to the pool, meeting women in the locker room and talking about work or men or how unresponsive their own bodies were despite all the physical exertion they put them through.

But today, Carrie couldn't even change in front of those other women. Instead, she slipped into a nearby toilet stall, hurriedly pulling off her clothes and putting on her swimsuit.

She always dressed quickly now, and found herself avoiding the mirror when she was naked. She took no pride in her body any more. Perhaps if she had been fatter or uglier, she wouldn't have attracted his attention in the first place.

Or if she had been stronger, she could have beaten him to his knees, to a pulp even. She could have hit him and scratched him and punched him. She could have gotten away with nothing more than a bad memory to haunt her.

But she didn't fight him. Looking back, Carrie wasn't even certain if there had been an opening to attack him. But even if it had been possible, she was convinced she wouldn't have hit him. She was paralyzed, immobilized, by fear. She just wanted him to go away.

"It wasn't your fault," the rape counselor had said, and later, her best friend had added, "You wouldn't feel guilty if someone robbed you or hit your car. Why do you feel guilty because someone attacked you? You didn't do anything to deserve it. No one does."

But the guilt was there, affecting every part of her life. She found it impossible now to make decisions at work, and even had to take a leave of absence until she got back some measure of confidence.

As for her relationship with Jeff—well, things had been a bit rocky even before (and how long, she wondered, would it be before she stopped measuring time in her life as "before" and "after"?), but then they had grown much worse.

She couldn't undress in front of him. She felt soiled, unclean. And sex—that was out of the question. Just the thought of it was enough to make her physically ill. What had once been a pleasurable experience had now come to mean submission, degradation, pain.

Carrie didn't blame him for leaving her, but she wished she could make him understand. Or was *she* the one who needed to understand and come to terms with what had happened?

No. She didn't want to think about it now. That wasn't why she had come here.

Carrie stepped off the ladder onto the pool floor and felt a bit more at ease in the water. Stretching a few times, she could feel the tension beginning to ease. Usually, once her muscles had warmed up, she would practice her dives, enjoying that brief period of flight before she slipped into the water.

She ought to go now to the deep section and dive in— right in, over her head—where the only thing that stood between her and drowning was her own strength. She ought to test herself, find out if any of the confidence she once had still remained.

But she was afraid and postponed the challenge a bit longer, settling for crisscrossing the width of the pool where the water was just under six feet in depth. Perhaps she shouldn't push herself. Her parents told her to take it easy, had even suggested she come home for a while.

"We'll take care of you," her mother had said, once she stopped crying. "It'll be like having our little girl back again."

"I told you that you were working too hard, keeping too many late nights," her father added gruffly. She heard the unspoken criticism: "If you had been home where a woman belonged, he wouldn't have been able to hurt you."

Was it her fault, she wondered? And if it wasn't, why did she feel so guilty?

"Will you be swimming much longer?"

It was the lifeguard, a young girl wearing a T-shirt over her swimsuit. She was holding a textbook and clearly wanted to get back to her studying. "Not that I want to rush you, but finals, you know, and I need to get to the library." She looked at her watch pointedly, and then gestured to the deserted pool. "Once you're done, I'm allowed to leave."

"I'm sorry," Carrie answered automatically and flushed. There it was, guilt again, but she was *allowed* to be here, she was *allowed* to be swimming, wasn't she? It wasn't *her* fault if there was no one else there or if the lifeguard had finals. There was no rational reason to feel guilty, and yet she did and apologized again.

"I won't be much longer," she said, even though she had originally planned to stay at least forty-five minutes.

"Okay, great," and the girl walked back to her chair where she buried her nose in her book and waited for Carrie to finish.

Six months ago, she wouldn't have felt guilty, but now she did. Six months ago, she would have told the girl that she'd be through in forty-five minutes and gone on to swim as she had planned. Six months ago, she wouldn't have cared or apologized or felt ashamed.

Carrie realized that, and realized too that the worst thing that man had done to her wasn't to violate her body. No, he had done more. He had destroyed her spirit, her sense of worth. The visible reminders had gone, and God willing, she would suffer no long-term physical effect of what had happened to her.

But the damage to her confidence was deep; the bruises to her mind weren't healing at all. She needed to reclaim some measure of confidence before the recovery process could begin, before she could say out loud, *scream* at the top of her lungs, "It wasn't my fault!" and believe it.

She climbed back up the metal ladder and walked to the deep end, near the lifeguard chair.

"Are you done?" the girl asked hopefully, but Carrie just shook her head. She had to start somewhere, and this was as good a place as any.

The diving board bounced a bit under her feet as she walked to the end. But she kept her balance, and even experimented a bit, pushing down with her toes and feeling the board spring back, almost catching her off-balance.

She put her arms out to hold herself steady, and bounced again, harder this time, and still she didn't fall, but descended and rose smoothly, rhythmically, confidently.

One final push and she was up in the air, above the water, then entering the water, sinking deep into the chlorine depths and suffocating, stifling, drowning. It was like that night all over again and she couldn't breathe, couldn't get away and why was it happening just when she felt so strong? And it hurt—God, her chest hurt so bad from holding all that air!—and she was going to die and there was nothing she could do....

Then suddenly, she surfaced, broke free of the water to draw one ragged gasp of breath after another. And now the pain *wasn't* as bad and she *hadn't* drowned and sometimes fighting *wasn't* the answer and sometimes there *wasn't* an answer, but all that really mattered was going through it, getting past it, going on.

And *that* took fighting too.

"Are you okay?"

Carrie suddenly realized that the lifeguard was kneeling at the side of the pool.

"I thought you were drowning," her face creased with concern.

"I'm okay," Carrie gasped, and took a last deep breath before releasing her hold on the edge. "I'll be okay now," and she pushed away from the wall, swimming with strong, sure strokes through the water.

PERIPHERAL VISIONS AND OTHER STORIES

PERIPHERAL VISIONS

"Shoot." Lena caught sight of the sign pointing the way to the rest stop off I-77 almost a fraction of a moment too late. She turned the wheel too sharply, causing the right tires of her old Ford Escort to kick up bits of gravel from the shoulder, before she could navigate it safely onto the turnoff.

Shaking slightly, she slowed the car to a more sedate twenty-five-miles per hour before brushing the perspiration from her forehead.

"That was close," she said to no one in particular. Talking to herself was a habit she had acquired since her mother's passing. The young think older people talk to themselves because they are going senile. But when there is no one left to talk to, you have to talk out loud. Otherwise, the silence can be deafening. And after decades as a practical nurse where she routinely carried on conversations with patients simply to ease the sterile loneliness of the oncology ward, Lena knew the value of the spoken word even when there wasn't anyone around to answer.

She glanced up at her rearview mirror, hoping the blue highway patrol car that seemed to be shadowing her since she crossed into West Virginia hadn't caught her latest misjudgment. That's all she would need: flashing lights, a request that she show her driver's license, and then a trip to the police station, where they would no doubt confiscate her car and contact her niece Claire.

Claire. By now, Claire might have figured out what Lena was up to, but she still wouldn't be sure exactly where her aunt had headed. For who would expect a seventy-two-year-old woman who had never driven beyond the Kingsville city limits to drive the nine-hundred-plus miles from Ohio to Florida?

Not Claire, that's for sure. Claire would have expected Lena to be looking forward to her move to Golden Glow, to behave as the sane, sensible, and highly responsible maiden aunt she had always been.

"Not this time, though," Lena said aloud, as she checked the parking area for other cars, including any with the telltale light bar mounted on the roof and distinctive twin gold stripes on the side, before pulling into a parking spot. "For once in my life, I'm going to do what I want to do, instead of walking a straight line right up to the end."

That's the biggest problem with the world today, she thought as she gingerly slid out of the car, carefully stretching her back to work out the kinks. The pain that had plagued her shoulder was even worse than usual this morning, undoubtedly aggravated by too many hours behind the wheel.

She moved her body slowly, continuing her conversation aloud. "People walk around with blinders on just like horses, their eyes glued on the goal, the 'Big Picture.' There's no sidestepping, no walking off the beaten path, no road less traveled. You get ahead that way, it's true. But what if where you end up isn't where you should have gone?"

The West Virginia sunshine was welcoming and a darn sight better than the freezing northeast Ohio weather she had left behind almost four hours earlier. A wet, sleety snow had made the driving more than a little challenging, especially once she got on the interstate and had to contend with all the tractor-trailers that were crowding the roadway.

PERIPHERAL VISIONS AND OTHER STORIES

It wasn't until she had approached the Marietta–Williamstown Interstate Bridge that would take her over the Ohio River and into West Virginia that the weather improved and the horizon looked brighter. Lena didn't usually believe in omens but this time she took heart in the fact that across the border the sun was shining, the snow was non-existent, and that it would be a warmer, better place than the one she had left.

And now, safe in another state, even her back felt better—well, at least, compared to how it had felt all winter long. Of course, she knew that nothing would make it feel completely fine. Even the pills only dulled the edge of the pain, never relieving it entirely.

That's really what decided her on this trip. She was afraid that if she waited any longer, either her nerve or her body would betray her and she would spend what was left of her time—three months, maybe less, she judged—in the fluorescent confines of the nursing home or hospital.

The whole time her niece Claire was talking—laying out stage after stage for her aunt as though Lena couldn't put two and two together and end up with four—Lena's mind flashed to tantalizing pictures of a bit of sand and sparkling water. It looked mighty appealing to her, especially since she was tired of shoveling snow from the driveway before she could get in her car and leave the house. It was a good car, even if it was as old as dirt, and she thought it deserved better than to have its fenders frozen off for weeks on end.

For that matter, so did she.

"You'll like the new place, Aunt Lena," Claire had said during her last visit. As usual, her niece had given the house a quick walk-through, her nose wrinkled slightly, her sharp eyes darting from side to side. Lena didn't know what the purpose of the inspection was. To check that there weren't any containers of moldy food or unwieldy piles of newspapers? To verify that Lena still had most of her marbles still rolling around inside her head? Did she think that, just because Lena was in her seventies, she wasn't competent anymore?

"They play bingo almost every day," she added, as though that was a plus.

Bingo—a game Lena detested. When her mother was alive, Lena had had to take her to the church bingo game every Friday night and then spend hours double-checking her choices to make sure she didn't make a mistake. No, Lena had no intention of whiling away what little was left of her life playing bingo at the "elder care facility"—a more politically correct name than old folks home but basically meaning the same thing after all.

Peculiar habit people have. They dress up the situation with a new name as though to make it more palatable. But in the end, it's just the same.

Lena had let Claire do the talking and then, after her niece left, sat down to evaluate her choices. She could do what Claire wanted: put the house up for sale, move into Golden Glow or whatever that place was called, and finish her life still following the straight-and-narrow.

Or for once in her life, Lena could focus so firmly on the image in her peripheral vision that it became all she could see: that sparkling water, that bit of sand.

"And why not?" she asked, as she pulled the old comforter out of the back seat to lay it on the seat of a nearby wooden picnic table. It was the perfect spot—still in full sun but close to the miniature dogwoods and redbuds, the white and purple-red blossoms giving her senses something to enjoy. "Where is it written that people our age have less of a right to follow their dreams than the twenty-somethings crowding the roadways of life? We've been here longer, given up more, been the responsible adults they expected us to be. When is it *our* turn?"

And there was no question that Lena *had* been the responsible adult. With no husband or children to care for, she had chosen a respectable career in nursing, going home each night to her small apartment close to the hospital. And then, when her mother grew too ill and eccentric to be left alone, Lena had acceded to her sister Mavis's request, retiring at sixty-two from her job to become the unpaid caretaker of her widowed parent.

"After all," her sister had pointed out with more accuracy than tact, "you live alone. You don't have anyone else"—which was true but Lena would have preferred that she hadn't been quite so blunt about it—"whereas I have my husband and my home to look after."

So that was how the next decade of Lena's life was decided for her. She gave up her apartment and her job, moved back home, and in some ways she hadn't truly minded. She loved her mother and grieved to see the old woman lose her grasp on reality. But the predictability of the days and nights was almost suffocating. Bingo once a week, church on Sundays—even the meal plan was set in stone, from the pot roast and boiled potatoes and carrots on Sunday to the beef soup Tuesday night and cod with macaroni and cheese on Friday.

Even at her worst, even when the Alzheimer's had robbed her of the ability to recognize Lena's face or remember her name, her mother had somehow managed to keep mental hold of the menu and would fuss if Lena deviated from it.

"Where's my fish?" she would complain, her thin voice trailing off as she looked at her plate. "It's Friday—where is my fish? We *always* have fish on Friday. Where's my fish?"

For ten long years, Lena watched her mother fade away into some place where she couldn't be reached, wondering if her mother knew what was happening to her mind, if somewhere behind all the damage the disease had wrought, some brain cells still remembered what normal was like, how it had been when her thoughts were under her control.

Maybe. Maybe not. But what Lena did know was that she would never willingly put herself in the same situation. And when her mother passed away right after Thanksgiving, and then unexpectedly, her sister just two months later, Lena wasn't sure at first what she should do or where she should go. Should she let her niece dictate her future: sell off her mother's household furnishings, put the old house on the market and tamely enter the confines of Golden Glow? Or should she finally break free, kick over the traces and gallop off into the Florida sunset?

When the notion first came to her, actually while she was accepting condolences at her sister's funeral, Lena dismissed it as a crazy idea. But then she realized that this was her last chance, a God-given opportunity to take her life in her hands. Things had changed for Lena and she wanted—no, she *needed*—to follow that change to the end.

Lena's share of her mother's life insurance plus her own savings would take care of the practical aspects of the plan. There was enough to get her where she wanted to go, somewhere where there was a bit of sand and sparkling water, somewhere that wasn't cold and dark.

PERIPHERAL VISIONS AND OTHER STORIES

But where should she go? She had never gone on vacation, never gone anywhere farther than her own backyard. And in the end, Lena wasn't entirely sure why she settled on Florida except that the thought of heat and sunshine was irresistible, especially after the harsh winter weather the area had endured and the even harsher verdict she had received two days after her sister died.

The entire time the doctors were talking of surgery and radiation and prognosis—the last just their way of saying "guess"—Lena was thinking of the patients she had cared for: the bald-headed, nausea-suffering shells of their former selves. Too many times medicine didn't help but only finished the job cancer had started, destroying what was left of their lives.

"Excuse me, gentlemen," she had finally said when she could get a word in edgewise, "just exactly what are your plans here?"

And just as she suspected, they had lots—all of them with one goal in mind which was success for them—*if* Lena was cooperative and didn't die. The route was laid out, clear and simple. All she had to do was leave the driving to them and they'd get her to the appointed destination.

But everyone carefully avoided talking about the extent of the problem, forgetting that she had been around enough lab reports to know what "metastasized" and "terminal" meant, and how a patient's chances of survival are in opposite relation to the number assigned to the stage of the disease.

"Not for me," Lena had said after the last doctor's appointment. If she had to go (and of course she did—everyone *had* to go sometime), it would be in her own way and on her own terms, *and* in a place of her choosing, and at that moment, a vision of sparkling blue water and cool, white sands popped into her head.

Lena didn't tell Claire because, much as she hated to admit it even to herself, she was a little afraid of her niece. Claire might just find some way of circumventing her plans: take the car away or assume control over her bank account, admit her to the hospital or maybe even the psych ward against her will. Claire, like her mother, could be pretty formidable when she chose.

No. Instead Lena swore the doctors to secrecy, took their prescriptions for pain medicine, and let Claire talk and plan and organize—which is how she came to be driving away from the frozen town of Kingsville on the first day of spring.

Her intention was to reach St. Augustine by nightfall of the second day. It would take just around fifteen hours or so, not counting rest stops, according to the Triple A travel guide she had picked up at the secondhand bookstore. But she knew that she couldn't do the whole trip in one fell swoop. A cheap motel somewhere around Charlotte, North Carolina—that's where she would take her break.

As for food, she had packed a few cans of tuna, some bananas, crackers and a half-empty jar of peanut butter, buns and a package of hot dogs into the small cooler—one of the two decent prizes her mother had won at bingo. The other prize, a slightly crooked tabletop grill and leaking bag of charcoal, would make the trip as well.

That's all she needed, she figured—plus her medicine and five hundred dollars in tens and twenties, some of it hidden in her suitcase, with the rest tucked inside her wallet.

And once she arrived in Florida (assuming she managed to make the trip without getting lost, arrested or otherwise delayed), she figured she'd open a bank account and transfer the rest of the money from up north to down south, before finding a small apartment near the ocean. There she could spend her days relaxing in the sunshine and falling to sleep at night lulled by the sound of the waves. She didn't care what the place would look like. Judging by the increasing severity of the pain, she wouldn't be living there that long anyway.

No, she wasn't worried about leaving Ohio or arriving in the sunshine state. It was the in-between part that really tested Lena's mettle. The drive through her home state was more than a little nerve-racking, especially since Lena, used to the slower speed limit on city streets, was unaccustomed to highways filled with vehicles speeding by doing seventy. She hugged the far right lane and drove along at a more sedate fifty-five miles an hour, trying to ignore the exasperated honking and occasional obscenity directed at her. Through snow, then icy rain, she continued, her blue eyes glued to the road and her hands glued to the wheel: at three and nine o'clock, just as she had been taught so many decades before. All she wanted was to cross the Ohio border. Then, she would feel like she was well and truly on her way to whatever the future held.

It wasn't until she had crossed into West Virginia that the first evidence of spring appeared. Along the interstate, the branches of the redbuds and dogwoods had begun to swell with life, the buds appearing magically where, a few weeks earlier, only barren twigs had been. She took a deep breath, realizing for the first time just how tense she had been, and decided it was safe enough to stop at the next area. She needed a bathroom, and, more importantly, she needed to take half a pill—just enough to take the edge off but not so much that she would be too drowsy to drive.

And by the time she came to the rest area at mile marker 165, it was clear from the occasional call of the warblers and whip-poor-wills that Lena could hear even through the closed car window that spring had indeed arrived. And if there was any doubt, the absence of snow and warmth of the sunshine told her that winter was well and truly behind her.

After a much-needed visit to the bathroom, Lena headed over to an empty picnic table, where she could take a break from worrying about the trucks, her niece and what had set her on this trip in the first place. Closing her eyes, she breathed in that fresh spring air that made her think of a very clean house and relaxed in the peace and quiet. Little by little, the tension and fears that crowded her mind faded away.

I'll be like the breeze, she thought sleepily. I'll just keep on moving, over and through whatever is in my path. And I'll get to my destination, even though I don't know what I'll find when I arrive.

She'd only been dozing for an hour or so when she awoke to feel something like wet sandpaper rubbing against her cheek. Raising her heavy lids, she was confronted by a pair of pop-bottle green eyes looking back at her with utter trust and complete independence—a combination of emotions only a cat can manage.

Lena lifted the scrawny kitten from the top of the picnic table, feeling its ribs through the matted black fur. He was young, barely weaned, and obviously either orphaned or abandoned. If it was the latter, Lena, while disappointed in finding yet another evidence of man's heartlessness, wasn't surprised. Years of working in the hospital had exposed her to a variety of inhuman acts that should be unthinkable in modern civilization. Babies abandoned in trash bins and toilets, "mistakes" discarded like yesterday's trash. Old people with their dignity and freedom of choice stripped from them, leaving them naked and defenseless in a world where modern medicine is God with the doctors as high priests.

Lena couldn't do anything about the rest of the world, but she could do something about this particular victim. She pulled herself to her feet and carried the cat to the car, intending to find something in her bag of food to feed it and herself, realizing for the first time how hungry she was. A can of tuna would do, she thought, and took it along with crackers and peanut butter and a few paper plates back to the table. There, she spread out the meal components, while the kitten rubbed hard against her legs, purring like a well-tuned racer. After dumping the tuna onto the plate, she set it on the ground and then sat back to watch the thin animal eat what must have been, to his eyes at least, a veritable feast of fish, while she munched on her cracker-and-peanut-butter sandwich.

It didn't take long for him to finish the food and then clean himself thoroughly, head to tail, the way cats do. Then he leaped back onto the table, where he waited for her to finish her meal, his sharp eyes marking her every move. Obviously, he had no intention of leaving her side. She recognized that fact, and after disposing of the plates and can in the trash, she carried him back to the car, where he curled sleepily into a small furry ball on top of the bag of charcoal briquettes.

"What am I going to do with you?" Lena said aloud, but clearly, the choice was made. Whether she wanted it or not, she now had a companion. Well, she had never had a pet before, she thought, as she shoved the comforter back into the car before taking her place once again behind the wheel and pulling out of the rest stop. In retrospect, there were a lot of things she'd never had. With luck, she might have enough time left to enjoy at least a few of them.

As for the kitten, he had clearly made his choice, catnapping for the next several hours, not waking when Lena stopped each time to pay the two-dollar tolls or even when the warm sunlight was replaced by the cold fluorescent illumination of the East River Mountain Tunnel. It was a relatively short tunnel, just a bit over a mile in length, but long enough to remind Lena of when she underwent an MRI, when the word "cancer" was starting to replace "arthritis" when the doctors discussed the cause of her shoulder pain.

She knew what an MRI was like, had talked to plenty of patients on her unit who had gone for one, but somehow knowing wasn't much help when you were the one sliding into the tube, holding your breath, literally and figuratively, until the test was done and the results were in.

She gripped the steering wheel and concentrated on the road ahead of her, as cars flashed by on her left, trying hard not to let the irrational fear that the tunnel would go on and on and she would never leave overtake her.

When she finally emerged from the tunnel into the sunlight, she breathed a shaky sigh of relief and wiped the perspiration from her forehead. "One down, one to go," she said aloud, and the sound of her voice woke the kitten, who jumped onto the back ledge to look at the passing surroundings. Everything met his approval, it seemed, until they entered the shorter Big Walker Mountain Tunnel. His responses were far more extreme and certainly more volatile than Lena's. Racing back and forth along the back ledge, he glared out the windows, hissed at the lights and the passing cars, making it quite clear that he opposed the entire idea that he was now confined in relative darkness.

In a way, distracting as it was, it took Lena's mind off her own fears, and she found herself amused by his behavior. And once they made it through and back out into daylight, she was pleased to realize that she had weathered the short span better than the first one. And certainly better than the kitten, who, exhausted from his energetic battle, now lay on the seat next to her, his chest heaving, while he shot her a glance making it clear that this had better be the last time he would have to undergo such an objectionable experience.

The kitten spent the next several hours riding on the ledge in the back window, alternately sharpening his claws on what was left of the upholstery and hissing at the cars following them. It wasn't until Lena had crossed into North Carolina and approached Exit 11 that it occurred to her that her traveling companion might be in need of a sandbox.

"What do you say, Cat?" she asked. "Should we find a place to stay for the night or keep on driving?"

As if in response to her question, the kitten hopped onto the front seat, settling down on the roadmap to wash himself, thereby blocking her view of the highlighted route. Clearly, it was time to find a place to stay, somewhere small and inexpensive, especially since it had started to rain, making it hard for Lena to see the road ahead. The kitten needed larger confines than the car in which to roam and Lena needed to lie down, take a pill, and hope that it worked well enough to allow her to finish the drive on the morrow.

The lighted vacancy sign at the Queen City Inn loomed up in the misty darkness. Despite its name, it didn't look very regal, thought Lena, just a small motel office with a row of doors leading to what would probably be tiny, airless rooms. But compared to the even smaller space of the car, it would be more than enough for Lena's needs.

"Just one person for the night," she answered in response to the desk clerk's questions, not seeing a need to mention her furry passenger. "And could you tell me where the nearest grocery store is?" she added as an afterthought, realizing that human food, while clearly palatable, was not exactly the best fare for a kitten's digestive tract.

"Down the road a bit," he answered, handing over the key after she gave him the $39.99 in cash. "Checkout's eleven a.m. sharp," he called after her, as she headed back to the car.

Luckily the U-Bag-It was close by and relatively empty, no doubt because of what had now become a downpour. She found a parking spot near the door, and, warning Cat to stay put, headed into the store in search of the pet food aisle.

The array of canned cat food was bewildering—everything from chicken and shrimp to steak and eggs. No wonder old people buy cat food, Lena thought. The selection was better than what was available for humans.

She chose several varieties, all conveniently equipped with pull-top lids, and then a two-section container for food and water, a bag of scented cat litter and a thirty-two quart plastic bin with a tight-fitting cover to serve as the litter box. Then she caught sight of the cat collars. Red and blue and green vinyl, adorned with cheap plastic jewels and gold-toned bells—ridiculous, unnecessary, and completely irresistible.

Shaking her head at her own extravagance, Lena added a green one the same shade as Cat's eyes to the small stack of supplies before heading to the checkout.

Back at the motel, she snapped the new collar around his neck, opened a can of food for him and dumped some litter into his portable bathroom. Then, swallowing her pill, she lay down on the bed to wait for it to take effect. And really, the pain wasn't all that bad, either because the weather had grown warmer the farther south she traveled, or because she wasn't sitting home alone, staring at the four walls.

Or maybe it was just the feel of the kitten who, once he had finished his feast, had curled up next to her, his back warm against her hip. The motel mattress might be lumpy but it beat lying in a hospital bed with tubes stuck in her and radiation burning out what was left of her insides.

With a final glance around the room, Lena shut off the bedside lamp and, pulling the blanket over the two of them, fell into a peaceful, dreamless sleep.

The next morning, she was awakened by the unexpectedly familiar sound of the kitten, purring in her ear.

"Here, now," she said, pushing him away from her face while she rummaged for yet another can of cat food, "quit washing my face and clean your own."

Cat jumped next to her, watching carefully as she peeled back the lid. While he ate, she opened a can of peaches and popped the slices, one by one, into her mouth. Not the kind of breakfast she would ordinarily have and certainly not the menu selection available at Golden Glow. But the sweetness of the fruit helped wash away the bitterness of last night's medication, although nothing could ever really take the taste away.

It was warmer—certainly a lot nicer than it would have been back in Ohio, she realized as she loaded the kitten, the litter and the few other items back into the car. By ten o'clock, she and the cat were on the interstate, enjoying the balmy temperatures that, by lunchtime, reached close to sixty.

"By dinnertime, Cat," she said aloud. The kitten looked up at her voice, which came out all cracked after such a long silence. Lena cleared her throat and said it again. "By dinnertime. We'll be in Florida by six, with plenty of time to watch the sun set over the ocean."

And they would have made it too if, just past the weigh station on I-95, Lena hadn't caught a glimpse of the young girl standing by the roadside, holding her thumb out in a scared way like she wasn't sure if she wanted anyone to stop or not. She looked barely out of her teens, but her belly hung out as big as a watermelon.

Lena shook her head and for just a second, hesitated. The girl was undoubtedly running away, and judging by her size, she was ready to have the baby at any minute. That could lead to all sorts of complications. Besides, Lena had her plan all figured out and a pregnant hitchhiker wasn't part of it. Nevertheless....

Resignedly, Lena slowed the car until she could safely pull over. The young girl grabbed her backpack and waddled as fast as she could to the car. Her face was streaked and dirty, and under the sunburn, she looked white and exhausted.

"Do you want a ride?" Lena asked, leaning over to open the door while simultaneously pulling Cat out of the way. The girl slid into the seat, dumping her bag onto the floor where Cat proceeded to sniff at it with interest.

"Get back with you," Lena said to him, heaving him head first into the back. "She doesn't have any tuna. How long have you been out there?" turning to the girl.

"I don't know, ma'am," she whispered in a soft Georgia drawl as she sank into the seat as though she didn't have enough energy left to draw a breath let alone form a thought.

"I'm going to Florida. Where are you heading?"

"I don't... Florida's fine," she said faintly, adding as an afterthought, "Thank you, ma'am," her voice trailing off as though speaking was simply too much effort.

"What's your—" but after another glance at her passenger, Lena gave up trying to get any more information. The girl was already fast asleep, or at least pretending awfully well. She didn't even move when Cat caught at a strand of her blonde hair as it moved in the breeze. Lena reached over and moved her satchel so she'd have more room for her legs, and then considered this latest turn of events.

If she had been paying attention to the road ahead, she might have passed the child too fast to notice her condition and the tired, scared look on her face. She wouldn't have to worry about a baby arriving unexpectedly or the girl's parents charging her with kidnapping or any of the other possibilities that could create problems.

If she had kept her eyes on the road and her mind on herself, she wouldn't have a frisky kitten *and* a pregnant girl to contend with.

Other people, Claire for instance, would have pulled into the nearest police station and dropped off at least one of these two, but Lena wasn't Claire. There must have been a reason for the girl to be where she was at that particular moment, right where Lena could catch a glimpse of her out of the corner of her eye. So for now, the pair had stretched itself to become a trio—all three in search of something better.

"My name's Sarah Jean."

Her voice startled Lena. She looked over at her and noticed that the girl had gotten a little color back, and the tense lines around her mouth had almost smoothed away.

At that moment, Sarah Jean's stomach rumbled and she blushed self-consciously.

"When did you last eat?" Lena asked, scanning the road for signs of a rest stop. At nine months, the bladder just couldn't be relied on.

"Oh, I'm not hungry," she protested.

"Maybe not, but the baby probably is, and if *you* don't eat up, there won't be a thing in you for him."

Just ahead, Lena caught sight of the blue Rest Area sign and she took the exit, hoping the rest stop wouldn't be crowded. They made a pretty strange group: an old lady, a very pregnant girl and one kitten, all stuffed into an old car with out-of-state plates. She definitely didn't want to explain any of this to anyone, least of all a nosy and highly official state patrolman.

Fortunately, the parking lot held just a few trucks, with the drivers taking their welcome breaks before getting back on their routes.

"There's a section for pets over there," Sarah Jean pointed out, and Lena headed in that direction, looking for a space that would be the shortest possible distance to the rest rooms. Then, she helped Sarah Jean out of the car and walked with her to the bathroom. No point in having her fall down and hurt herself, Lena thought, falling back into her familiar caregiver role.

"I've got some hot dogs and a grill," Lena said as she waited for the girl to exit the stall. "I can make us a meal if I remembered the matches."

"I've got some," Sarah Jean said, pushing open the door. She rummaged through her bag, pulling out a cigarette case. "Oh, I gave them up," she said quickly, in answer to Lena's raised eyebrows. "It was hard but I knew the baby needed me to."

She opened the case and showed the inside to Lena. No cigarettes—just a pack of matches, a few dollar bills and her driver's license. Lena reached in and before the girl could protest, pulled the license free. Sarah Jean Hopkins of Eulonia, Georgia, born in 1998. Well, that answered one question. As of last month, the girl was eighteen, which Lena hoped was legal age in Georgia.

She handed back the license without a comment and Sarah Jean shoved it into her purse, saying resentfully, "I would have told you if you had asked. And I'm old enough to—"

"Nobody is old enough to be all alone on the highway with nowhere to go and a baby ready to come," Lena interrupted tartly, and then turned to go back to the car. Sarah Jean stood there, uncertainty written on her face.

"Oh, come on," Lena said impatiently. "You can help me light the grill. I've never used it before."

Between the two of them, they moved the grill, the charcoal and the food over to the picnic table underneath a gazebo. While she waited for the coals to be hot enough— "You want them to be sort of gray looking and ashy," Sarah Jean explained—Lena opened another can of cat food, tuna this time, to distract the kitten who was nosing around the fire, his whiskers dangerously close to the glowing coals.

"Here, you," she said, laying the can on the table and setting him next to it, where she could keep an eye on him. "This time tomorrow we'll be catching your dinner right from the ocean."

Cat gave her a quick look but didn't look at all excited by the prospect. Maybe, thought Lena amusedly, he preferred his food already de-boned and bloodless.

Sarah Jean paced a few times, before slumping onto the bench to stare moodily into the fire.

"We were supposed to get married!" she finally burst out, not looking at Lena and shoving her hands deeper into the pockets of her tunic. "He'd promised to marry me when I told him I was pregnant. Then, pretty soon, he quit coming around and Mama said I was a disgrace and she said she'd send me up to live with Great-Aunt Edna until I had the baby. And I *hate* Great-Aunt Edna! She's always sniffing at me like I smelled or something," and here she burst into tears.

"Claire," Lena said without thinking, and Sarah Jean looked up in confusion, the tears leaving dirt streaks on her cheeks. "My niece Claire," she said by way of explanation. "She sniffs just like your great-aunt, like I'm a bag of dirty old clothes that needs to be scrubbed and hung out to dry. You're running away from your great-aunt and I'm running away from my niece," Lena added with a grin. "We make a quite a pair, don't we?" At that, Sarah Jean smiled tearfully.

"I guess you think I'm old enough to know better," she said, but Lena just shook her head.

"If there is one thing I know, it's that age doesn't make us old enough to know better. It's listening to the voice inside us that does that. If the voice told you Great-Aunt Edna was a bad idea, then it was probably right."

"It's not her fault," Sarah Jean said after a moment, like she was trying to be fair. "And it was probably not what she wanted either—an unmarried pregnant girl in her home. I might have even considered it except—" and here she paused.

"Except what?"

"They wanted me to give the baby up," she whispered, her hands sliding protectively over her belly. "They said I was too young to raise it and that they didn't want to deal with the responsibility. They said," and she swallowed hard, "they said it would be better if I didn't have it at all."

Lena was beginning to get a clearer picture of what had driven Sarah Jean onto the side of the road, and could only marvel that she hadn't left before this. It was obvious her parents had wanted her to get an abortion, and how she had defied them, Lena couldn't imagine. It wasn't just obstinacy—she could tell by the way she kept her hands crossed over her stomach that she wanted to protect this child, perhaps in the way that she herself had never been protected.

In any case, if she wanted to leave the coldness of her house and home, she was old enough to do so. And Lord knows Lena was old enough to help.

"Look, here's what we'll do," Lena said, wanting to give her something positive to focus on. "We'll find a place outside of Jacksonville to spend the night, and then bright and early tomorrow, we'll head over to St. Augustine. That's where I planned to stay," she explained. "Once we get there, we'll decide what to do next."

Sarah Jean nodded her head, her eyes showing more hope than Lena had seen in them until now. Then the young girl busied herself setting the hot dogs on top of the fire. "The coals are ready. Why don't you let me cook them while you rest?" She pulled her backpack out of the car to slip it under Lena's feet.

Lena nodded her head in thanks, the unexpected lump in her throat keeping her from voicing her appreciation. It had been a long time since anyone had spontaneously done something nice for her, and it was all the more welcome because of that, like a taste of water is so much sweeter when you're parched with thirst.

The hot dogs tasted quite good too, although Lena was certain that the nutritional value was not the highest. But she ate two and probably would have eaten another if a quick glance at her watch hadn't shown her there were only a few more hours until sunset.

"We had better get moving and find a place to stay," she said, and began loading the remains of the impromptu picnic back into the car. Sarah Jean dumped out the still smoldering coals and pushed dirt over them until the glow faded. Then she stowed the grill in the trunk, and taking her place in the front seat, she gathered Cat onto her lap. The two of them looked like they belonged together, and, truth to tell, the car seemed a warmer, friendlier place with traveling companions in it.

It wasn't long before they had crossed into Florida, and just on the outskirts of Jacksonville, Lena pulled into the first motel she found. Her shoulder had gotten much worse, but she didn't like to drive when the medication was taking effect. And

Lord knows, Sarah Jean was in no condition to be behind the wheel. Once in the room, the young girl fell asleep almost before her head hit the pillow, but it took Lena a little longer before the ache dulled enough to let her rest.

But she didn't mind now that she had something more to focus on than pain. Before today, Lena hadn't really cared how much time she had left. But now, she wanted to stay around just a bit longer. Life, it seemed, could still hold some surprises for her.

Lena let Sarah Jean sleep until almost noon, taking an unexpected pleasure in the regular sound of breathing coming from the next bed. Then she started packing up odds and ends, making just enough noise to penetrate the young girl's slumber without startling her awake. But it was Cat's playful nature that finally did the trick. He just couldn't resist the strands of hair that stretched across the pillow, and began tugging at them until Sarah Jean shooed him away.

"Lord, what time is it?" she asked, pushing herself up to as comfortable a position as her belly would allow. She tucked her hair behind her ears and then gave Lena a tentative smile. "You've been awfully good to me," she said, and then bent over to slip her shoes back on her feet, before continuing. "But I don't want you to think you have to look out for me. I can manage on my own."

She stood up and then almost immediately sat back down again. "Oh..." she said faintly, leaning back to rest her head on the pillow.

"You're probably hungry," said Lena, ignoring for the moment what Sarah Jean had just said. "Pull yourself together and we'll get something to eat. And then we can talk about everything later."

But somehow, in between ordering grits and eggs and feeding Cat and packing up the car, the conversation never took place. Instead, they took their accustomed places in the car—Lena behind the wheel, Sarah Jean with the map spread across what was left of her lap, and Cat sprawled on the bags in the back—and followed the interstate until, an hour later, they found themselves in St. Augustine.

"Now what?" asked Sarah Jean, as they turned onto Ponce de Leon Boulevard.

"I don't know," Lena admitted. "I guess I never got any farther in my mind than St. Augustine—well, St. Augustine and a beach and the ocean."

"Then the ocean it is," Sarah Jean said decidedly and pored over the map, looking for the best route to take them close to the water.

"Look," she said, her fingers tracing a path east of the city, "we can head over to Avenida Menendez and then cross the Matanzas Bay on something called the Bridge of Lions to Anastasia Island. 'Anastasia Island'—that has a nice sound, doesn't it? There has to be a beach somewhere on the island, don't you think? Maybe once we get there, we can drive around and find one that you like."

But as much as Lena would have liked to take her time and choose the one that most fit her mental image, the delay caused by the traffic over the two-lane bridge combined with the steadily increasing pain made it imperative that she find a place to stay and soon. She hadn't taken her pain pill, and needed one. Badly.

"Look," Lena said, as they reached the end of the almost sixteen-hundred-foot-long drawbridge, "there's a hotel right there." She turned left and pulled into the parking lot. "Wait here," and taking her purse from behind the backseat where Cat had been using it as a makeshift bed, she went through the double glass doors and into the lobby.

"Welcome to the Edgewater Inn," said the woman behind the desk. "My name is Christalene Benjamin. May I help you?"

"We need a room for a few nights. Two beds," Lena added, choosing not to mention Cat in case there was some prohibition against pets.

"We have a room available on the second floor," Christalene said, pushing the registration form across the counter for Lena to complete. "Or would you rather have the first? We don't have an elevator."

"First, I think," said Lena, since the thought of climbing stairs with suitcases in tow was more than she could handle. "And somewhere quiet—an end room, maybe?" just in case Cat decided to perform an impromptu solo.

"We've got one that just opened up: a lovely room with two comfortable double beds, mini-refrigerator and coffee-maker, a desk and a sliding glass door that leads to a patio and our little private beach area with a nice view of the bay and the St. Augustine skyline—beautiful in the evening! We have a continental breakfast in our lounge from 7:30 to 9:30 each morning and a social hour from five to six with refreshments and appetizers," and she paused to take a breath before asking, "How does that sound?"

Perfect, thought Lena, especially the bed part. All she wanted was to take her pill and lie down. "That's fine," realizing Christalene was waiting for an answer.

"Wonderful! I know you'll be comfortable," and she handed the key card to Lena. "Oh, and did I mention the lions?"

Startled, Lena looked up. Lions? Was there a circus nearby? She could just imagine how Cat would react hearing the roar of a much larger and certainly wilder feline.

"Oh, don't worry," she laughed. "They aren't real! They're granite! They were donated by a local couple, Wolfgang and Miki Schau, who wanted a match to the Medici lions at the west entrance to the bridge. *Those* two are called Firm and Faithful and these are named Peli and Pax for happiness and peace. The pair were installed in Davis Park just last July and we had a big celebration to welcome them!"

As interesting as the lion information was, Lena could tell that the innkeeper would keep on talking if she didn't interrupt her. And the longer she stood there, the worse the pain was becoming. She slipped the keycard into her handbag, but before turning away, asked, "Do you know of any place available to rent? I'm looking for an apartment—some place near the water," realizing after she said it that almost anywhere on the narrow island would be close to either the ocean or the bay.

Christalene beamed, ready to be of service yet again. "For how long? I only ask because a friend of mine has a place for rent, close to Crescent Beach on Cubbedge Road. She does six-month rentals and her last tenant just left. It's just about ten miles from here on A1A. Here, I'll write down the address and her phone number," and in just a few moments, Lena was in possession of the information. "Let me know if you need anything," Christalene called as Lena headed back out the door. "And have a good stay!"

"Everything okay?" Sarah Jean asked, and Lena realized she must have been worried. Maybe she thought Lena had changed her mind. Or maybe, now that she had finally stopped running, she was realizing the momentousness of her decision to leave home.

"Everything is fine," said Lena, carefully backing out of the parking spot to head down the driveway to their room. "Well, here we are, for now at least. Let's get inside and we can figure out what we're doing next. And keep him hidden," nodding toward the kitten. "I didn't mention him to the desk clerk."

"No problem," and Sarah Jean bundled him into her backpack like a ball of dirty laundry.

It didn't take long to empty the car—neither of them had much in the way of possessions—and once inside, both took off their shoes and sank back onto their respective double beds.

"Feels good to stretch out, doesn't it?" Lena said after a few minutes, but when there was no answer she looked over at the young girl and saw that she was fast asleep. Good, Lena thought, and she reached over to her handbag and pulled out her bottle of medicine. No need to answer any questions, and swallowing the pill, she rolled over onto her side and almost as quickly fell into a deep, dreamless sleep.

It was close to suppertime before she awakened to find Sarah Jean looking down at her.

"Lena, you okay?" her forehead creased in concern. "You were moaning a bit, like something hurt."

"Just a bad dream," and Lena forced herself to sit upright. The pain felt better, and for the first time in a long time, she actually felt hungry. "What do you say we get something to eat?"

"Great! I was looking at the brochures on the desk and there's a place called O'Steen's Restaurant just down the street. Do you want to walk?"

"That sounds great," said Lena. Perhaps a walk *would* help, might loosen the kinks and get the blood flowing. "Give Cat some food and then we'll head out."

They left the inn and walked down Anastasia Boulevard, reaching the restaurant in less than twenty minutes. Once there, they polished off more food than either had eaten in the past twenty-four hours: a delicious cup of Minorcan clam chowder with a little bite to it—"That's from the datil pepper," their waitress explained—and then a dozen fried shrimp apiece, followed by a generous slice of homemade coconut cream pie.

"Lord, I am stuffed!" said Sarah Jean, patting her belly. "But the food tasted so good, didn't it?"

"It did," agreed Lena, realizing that this was the first meal in a long time that she had enjoyed. Or maybe it wasn't the food so much as having someone to eat it with.

They took their time walking back to the hotel, and by the time they reached their room, the sun was setting. As comfortable as the beds looked, the lure of the deck bathed in sunset proved irresistible to both of them, and going out onto the deck, they settled themselves on the white wooden rocking chairs where they rested in companionable silence.

The view was everything that the innkeeper had promised. The old-fashioned bridge lamps were reflected in the water, while across the bay the lights from the restaurants outlined the city skyline like stars suspended on an invisible string. The rhythmic lapping of the waves onto the sand added to the sense of peacefulness. It was perfect—just what Lena had pictured so many weeks ago.

"Perfect," said Sarah Jean aloud, uncannily echoing Lena's thoughts. "So much better than back home," and Lena wasn't sure if she meant the location or just the freedom from fighting.

"Tomorrow, we'll check out the apartment the woman told me about," said Lena. "It's supposed to be near Crescent Beach, just down the main road a ways." She shivered a bit in the cool air, the slight breeze running across her unprotected arms.

"Do you want a cover or something?" Sarah Jean asked, but Lena shook her head.

"No, I think what we both need is a good night's sleep. You go in and use the bathroom and let me know when you're done," wanting just a little time to herself to think about her plans. And not just her plans but plans for Sarah Jean. The strong feeling of protectiveness that made her stop to pick up the girl on I-95 had grown quickly into something more maternal, and she wanted to make sure that whatever she decided to do for herself, the young girl and her unborn baby were equally cared for.

"I'm done," called Sarah, and Lena got to her feet, deciding to take half a pill before bed so she could get a good night's sleep.

After a quick breakfast of bagels topped with cream cheese in the lounge, Lena and Sarah Jean packed up the kitten and drove down Anastasia Boulevard, armed with the information the helpful innkeeper had provided and even more brochures about the area that Sarah Jean had collected from the display rack by the desk. At first, it looked like the island was all tourism-focused, with hotels, restaurants, bars, and souvenir shops practically right up against each other, while vacationers crowded the sidewalks. Lena was starting to question the wisdom of her idea. She had wanted peace and quiet and instead seemed to have chosen a place where neither existed until the wee hours of the morning.

But then, as she drove farther down the road and farther from the inn, traffic lessened and it looked less like a vacation spot and more like neighborhoods where kids could play and families could live.

"Look! There's a sign for Crescent Beach!" Sarah Jean said excitedly. "Can we go there first just to take a look?" and Lena turned left onto a sand-covered road, and then right into a parking lot.

"It even *smells* like the ocean," Sarah Jean said rapturously, rolling down her window and taking a deep breath. "I just want to go out on the beach, just for a second—okay?" and Lena nodded.

"Are you coming?" the young girl asked, sticking her head back in the car. Lena hesitated and then made up her mind. She hadn't driven all those miles to stay in the car. No, by God, she was going to go out onto the beach and breathe in that fresh ocean air.

She pulled the comforter from the back seat where they had left it last night and followed Sarah Jean up the short road and then down the sandy path to the beach. It was fairly deserted at that hour of the morning, the water probably too cold for most swimmers. With Sarah Jean's help, Lena spread the comforter onto the sand so the two of them could settle themselves comfortably.

"It's so quiet here," said Sarah Jean. "Like a church, almost."

And Lena knew what she meant. It was like a church. Or a holy place—a place of respite and peace. And if ever there were two people in need of sanctuary, it was herself and Sarah Jean.

The young girl sprawled on the blanket, spreading her fingers against her belly. "It feels so good to stretch out," she said but then frowned a bit. "He's not moving as much now. Do you suppose he's okay?"

"He's probably just getting ready to come out and see you," Lena answered, turning away from the girl. She needed to take a pill but didn't want Sarah Jean to see her do it. She'd start to worry, and, in her condition, it wouldn't do her a bit of good.

"You think so?" she asked eagerly, but then the excited look faded from her face. "I'm giving him up," she said flatly, not meeting Lena's eyes.

Lena looked at her thoughtfully. At her age, she considered herself a pretty good judge of character, and after all Sarah Jean had been through, Lena couldn't imagine why she'd made that decision now.

"Let's be reasonable," Sarah Jean said, and Lena wasn't sure if she was pleading with her or herself. "What can I offer him? I don't have a job, my family has thrown me out—what kind of life will he have?" and she burst into tears.

Lena waited a bit for her to stop weeping and dry her eyes, and then spoke with conviction.

"You think you don't have a choice but you're wrong. Now, wait—" and she held up a hand to stop Sarah Jean from interrupting. "You can only see one view, Sarah Jean. You're wearing blinders, just like everybody else. All you see is a fatherless baby and a husbandless mother and bills piling up. I'm not saying that isn't a true picture. It will be hard if you keep the baby. But what I want you to do is stop focusing on that one picture and see what else is there, somewhere just outside your line of vision. When you just think about the baby, Sarah Jean," and Lena leaned closer to her, putting all the persuasion she could into her voice, because this was so important, "what do you see?"

The young girl was quiet for a moment, and then said, "I see me holding him while he sleeps. I see him chasing a ball in the park and playing on the jungle gym."

"That's what you have to go after, Sarah Jean," Lena said softly but with determination. "That's *your* peripheral vision, and it's showing you what you might miss if you stick to this path, this new decision."

She sat back, gasping a bit because the pain had suddenly gotten very bad. Sarah Jean didn't notice, only lay there, soft-eyed and dreaming, perhaps seeing her little one on the first day of school.

"And it wouldn't be wrong of me to keep him?" she asked finally, but Lena shook her head.

"You just try to give him up and I'll smack you silly," she said, forcing a smile past the pain.

The young girl laughed, but then her laugh turned into a moan, as she clutched at her belly with both hands, her face suddenly white from strain.

"What's wrong?" but Lena knew what that look meant. The baby was ready to face the world, and it was up to them to get him born in a hospital, instead of on a sandy beach.

And they made it too, by the skin of their teeth, stopping long enough to drop Cat off in their room before crossing the Bridge of Lions to the mainland and the hospital. Lena helped Sarah Jean into the emergency entrance where she was quickly wheeled to the maternity area.

Then, while the young girl did her part to push the baby out, Lena rested in the waiting room, sipping cold water and worrying about her. Strange how close two people could get in a short space of time. Two days ago, she didn't even know a girl named Sarah Jean. All she could think about was getting to Florida and finding a place to die. Now her thoughts were occupied with other issues—like making some kind of provision for the young girl and her soon-to-be-born child.

"And why not?" she said to herself, trying to ignore the steadily increasing pain. "I don't have anyone to leave my money to. My sister is gone, and Claire has enough of her own. Why shouldn't Sarah Jean get it?"

All Lena would ask in return was that she would take care of Cat as long as she could—a simple request because the two of them had taken to each other like soul mates. Funny how things can change. Lena had been ready to give it all up—the trip itself had been her way of thumbing her nose at the prognosis—but since she'd met Sarah Jean, she wanted to stay on a bit more. For a moment, she let herself daydream about a little beach cottage, the sounds of a baby cooing, and a clothesline with little shirts and shorts flapping in the breeze.

Then the pain washed over her and the picture faded away. The last thing Lena heard, oddly enough since the hospital was miles from the sea, was the sound of the tide as it rolled onto the beach and then ran out again.

"Ma'am, ma'am, are you okay?"

Lena moaned a bit when someone shook her shoulder. She opened her eyes and saw a nurse looking at her, eyes full of concern.

"I'm fine, just a little tired," and she forced herself to smile.

"I just wanted to let you know that your granddaughter is doing just fine," and the nurse smiled at her.

For a minute Lena was confused. And then she realized Sarah Jean must have told them they were related. And in a sense they were, if love and concern had the same value as blood ties.

"She wants to see you," the nurse added, and helped Lena get to her feet. The two of them walked down to Sarah Jean's room, where the young mother was holding a tiny white bundle, looking for all the world like a Madonna with her child.

"Well, here he is!" and Sarah Jean turned the baby a bit so Lena could see his tiny face. "Charlie, here's your Grandma," and she glanced up at Lena who smiled back at her.

"Hey, young man," and she reached her fingers out to the baby, who grasped one firmly, pulling it toward his tiny mouth.

"No, no, your mama has something better for you." Gently Lena disengaged her finger. "So it looks like I had better get us settled into our new place pretty quickly. Tell you what, I'm going to head out now and check out that apartment and get a few things and then I'll be back later to see the two of you, okay?"

Sarah Jean smiled and nodded, then yawned so widely that Lena's jaw ached in response. The nurse took the baby and laid him in the crib. "You get some sleep, now," she said to the young girl, and then turned to lead Lena out the door. "You look like you could stand some sleep yourself. Why don't you come back later today, after six sometime, and then you two can visit," and Lena nodded.

She did need sleep, but first, she had to find a place for her rapidly expanding family to live as well as buy a crib and some other necessities for the baby.

"I'll be back later," she said to Sarah Jean, but the girl was already fast asleep.

It didn't take long to find what she needed and in short order the car held diapers, baby clothes, and a travel crib that would do for the first few weeks. Time enough to get the rest of the items once they were all in their new home. Then, before heading back to the inn, Lena drove back down to Cubbedge Road and after checking out the furnished two-bedroom apartment, made arrangements to move in the following day.

Once back at the inn, it was time to make a call to Ohio. She needed to put in place a few changes to her will and fortunately her attorney was also an old family friend who had been in Lena's confidence ever since she received her diagnosis.

"Here's where I'll be staying," she said, giving him the apartment's address after she told him what amendments she wanted. "Send the papers down by express mail and I'll get them notarized and back to you. And not a word to Claire," she reminded him.

Once that call was finished, she fed the kitten and then headed to the car. It was still a little early to go back to the hospital, so after crossing the bridge, she drove around a bit, taking note of the locations for the grocery store, pharmacy, and church, before finally ending up in front of the Fountain of Youth.

Was that what had brought her to this city? Somewhere deep inside did she harbor a dream that taking a sip from the fountain would change everything? No, she thought to herself. She was realistic enough to know that the path was laid out for her and that it was a short one indeed. But still, it couldn't hurt to visit the fountain. Men had traveled farther than she in search of life.

She paid her entry fee and walked down the path to the springhouse, passing the fenced area where the peacocks strutted and scratched at the ground, occasionally spreading their feathers in a brilliant display of blue and green. To Lena, more familiar with the cardinals, bluebirds, and goldfinches back home, there was something exotic about these birds, even if their cries seemed to have more in common with the raucous call of the blue jay than what one would expect given their beautiful coloring.

Inside the springhouse, the flagstone floor and coquina walls combined to keep the space cool and quiet. Cautiously, Lena made her way down the few steps to the spring itself and, taking a cup from the nearby table, leaned forward to fill it with the water that came all the way from the aquifer miles below. It was cool and refreshing, and Lena drank it all and then refilled the cup, carrying it back up the steps as carefully as though it were the Holy Grail.

Sitting on the bench in the corner, she sipped the spring water and thought about how much had changed. Time itself had changed—or maybe it was her definition of time. When she left Ohio, she was counting down her life in terms of months, knowing the end was approaching and not really minding as long as she made it to her destination. A journey to death was how she had envisioned it, but now it turned out to be a journey to life—a new life—a life with Sarah Jean and Cat and now baby Charlie. And she wanted to make the most of it, make the most of the *time* left to her, before her journey ended.

"You know, most people call it the Fountain of Youth but we also say it's the Spring of Eternal Hope."

Startled, Lena looked up. She had been so lost in her thoughts that she hadn't realized that one of the tour guides had come into the springhouse.

"Some people are hoping for youth," the guide went on, as she added a few more cups to the stack on the table, "and others just hoping for something better. What about you? What did you hope for when you drank from the spring?"

Lena just smiled and shook her head, and the guide smiled back, before leaving the small room. She finished the water, wondering about those who believed that a glass or two would add years to their life. But it's not just about living longer, Lena knew, but about making the most of the time you have: years, months or even just days. And not just *living*, but being truly alive. That's how she felt now—as though she had never really lived before—and for that, she had Sarah Jean and young Charlie to thank.

She placed her cup carefully in the trash bin and then made her way back to the car to see the newest addition to her family. And before Sarah Jean and her son were discharged, Lena had moved their few belongings to the small apartment across the road from the beach. Maybe it was just her innate sense of responsibility or maybe the spring water had had a positive effect on her energy level, but Lena was able to get all the items on her to-do list checked off in short order. Money talks, and with the cash she had brought with her, she was easily able to hold up her end of the conversation, even arranging for the baby furniture to be delivered in twenty-four hours.

"It's beautiful," Sarah Jean breathed, walking around the tiny bedroom, running her fingers on the cushioned top of the changing table and peering into the closet, where stacks of diapers, sleepers and tiny socks were lined up neatly on the shelves. "But the money—it must have cost you a fortune!"

"Don't worry about it," and Lena waved her hand, trying not to notice the sharp pain. By now she should be used to it. It wouldn't be so bad if she took the medicine as prescribed, but she had other plans for the pills. "Let me hold the baby." She sat in the white wicker rocker, reaching out her arms for the sleeping bundle.

Once in Lena's arms, Charlie opened his blue eyes wide and fixed them on her, as though he wanted to remember her for the rest of his life.

"Pretty baby," Lena said foolishly, and reached one finger out for him to hold.

"You know, Lena, I think this has all been too much for you. You look, well, tired or something," Sarah Jean said, coming closer to her. "Maybe the trip was too much and then all this. I think you ought to see a doctor."

"No need, really. I'll be fine if I take it easy," said Lena, amused and touched by the girl's assumption of authority. Maybe having a baby had given her a healthy dose of maternal feelings, but Lena could hardly imagine a more unlikely chick for Sarah Jean to mother-hen than her.

"So what's the plan?" asked Sarah Jean, settling herself on the floor, her spine resting against Lena's leg. As if responding to a signal, Cat came over and curled in her lap, purring contentedly.

"No plans, little mother," and Lena freed her finger from the baby long enough to pat the top of Sarah Jean's head. "We have a place to stay and that's all that matters."

"But now there's the baby," and then Sarah Jean stopped, and blushed. "I'm sorry. It's not your problem. *We're* not your problem. Look, maybe you ought to stay here, and the baby and I will go back home. You won't get any rest with him fussing all the time."

"Now, you listen," and Lena grabbed her hair, tugging at it until the girl half-turned to face her. "You and I didn't travel all this way to split up now. Let's just play it by ear, and see what turns up. I have some money set aside and we'll be fine. Besides," she laughed as the baby gurgled at her, "maybe what these old bones need is someone like little Charlie here to make them flexible again."

Sarah Jean smiled, and then turned back, leaning her head lightly against Lena's knee and dozed off. The baby closed his eyes, and pretty soon, Lena was the only one awake in the room.

With Sarah Jean and Charlie now at home, the three of them fell into a comfortable routine. As if to make up for what his young mother had gone through before his arrival, Charlie was a model baby, eating, sleeping, and smiling with welcome regularity. During the day, Lena and Sarah Jean took turns playing with the infant, and at night, when Sarah Jean would wake to nurse him, Lena would sometimes steal into the room to watch the two of them, silhouetted in the moonlight, before going back to her bed. She had no wish to intrude on their private time.

"We have a good life, don't we, Lena?" Sarah Jean asked several weeks later as she rinsed out Charlie's bib. Lena nodded, dangling a set of plastic fish over the baby chair while Charlie bounced and cooed. "I never would have thought that it would end up like this," she continued, coming over to stand beside the two of them, resting one hand lightly on Lena's shoulder.

Lena winced and moved slightly, just enough to let Sarah Jean's hand fall away. These days, even the slightest touch was painful.

"I'm sorry," Sarah Jean said in surprise. "Did I hurt you?"

"No, really, it's all right. I must have wrenched it a bit when I was getting out of bed. These old bones, you know," said Lena, using the same old excuse she always did, but this time Sarah Jean was not so easily appeased.

Her brow furrowed and she said, "I still think you ought to see the doctor. There are things they can do, even if it's arthritis...." Her voice trailed off and she looked at Lena anxiously.

"Don't be silly," Lena answered firmly. "A body doesn't get to be this old without aches and pains. Besides, right now, you need to get the two of you ready. Today's Charlie's six-week appointment, you know."

"I know," but Lena could tell by Sarah Jean's voice that the subject wasn't closed. Well, she would take her mind off it by baking a chocolate cake in honor of Charlie's six-week birthday. When the two of them got back, Lena would put six candles on it and then together they could blow them out. Lena had taken to manufacturing reasons to celebrate, reasoning that there would be precious few opportunities in the months ahead if the pain was any indication of the progression of the disease.

While the cake cooled on the rack, Lena wrote a note for Sarah Jean so she'd know where to find her and then slowly walked across the way to the beach, carrying the beach chair she'd picked up at a garage sale. She'd wait there for the two to return. It was too beautiful to stay inside.

The beach was deserted, although there were footprints on the white sands left behind by an earlier beachcomber. Soon, Lena thought, the tide will wash them away. But just because they no longer existed didn't mean that they were never there. It was the same with people. Even when they are gone, they still leave behind footprints of a sort—impressions on other lives, other minds, other hearts. There was a time when Lena thought her life would end with her death. But now, God willing and if she did it right, she would live on in a way through Sarah Jean and young Charlie.

She lowered herself onto the chair and closed her eyes, dozing until, sometime later, she was awakened by the crunch of footsteps. Sarah Jean came over to join her, laying the sleeping infant in his carrycot on the sand next to her.

"How's our boy doing?" she asked, but Sarah Jean was silent. Lena glanced at her, seeing that her face was more serious than it had been since the baby was born.

"Why are you taking pain pills?"

The question startled her, and, for a moment, Lena wasn't certain what to say. She reached over and twitched the corner of Charlie's blanket, smoothing it out. The baby's cheeks were rosy from the Florida sunshine. He'll be a handsome young boy, Lena thought, and an even handsomer man. I wish....

"Lena, I asked you a question. What are those pills for?"

"How do you know what they are?" Lena was stalling for time and they both knew it. But Sarah Jean answered her anyway.

"I asked the druggist when I picked up Charlie's vitamins. You know, the young one down at the corner. He told me."

Lena knew whom she meant. The good-looking young pharmacist—the one who always had time to spare when Sarah Jean came into the store. He was kind and soft-spoken, and really seemed taken with her, even though she had a baby and no husband. And he wasn't married. Lena had asked.

"I wasn't spying," she added, with a sidelong look at her. Perhaps she thought Lena was angry. "I found them when you asked me to bring you a handkerchief out of your top drawer. Lena, please tell me what's wrong. I can take it, you know. I'm not a child."

She was right, Lena knew. She *wasn't* a child, not any more. When they first met, just a few short weeks ago, she *had* been a child—a very frightened, very pregnant one. But since she had the baby, she had changed. Motherhood had brought her new confidence, self-assurance, and a maturity that sat well on her narrow shoulders.

No, Sarah Jean wasn't a child anymore. She deserved to know the truth.

"Well, the fact of the matter is," Lena said casually, "I have a cancer. A rather fast-growing one. And the pills are supposed to help with the pain. Not that it's been too bad," she added quickly. "But every now and then, I need one."

Sarah Jean was silent, and when Lena looked over at her, she saw her face had grown rather white. Lena took her hand.

"Don't worry about it," she said, trying to cheer her up. "At my age, it was bound to be something anyway. Besides, it's no big thing."

"No big thing!" Sarah Jean burst out, snatching her hand away and glaring at her. "No big thing!" she repeated. "And just when were you planning on telling me about this? No, it just isn't right," she continued. "And what do the doctors say? Let me guess—you aren't seeing a doctor. Lena, what do you think you're *doing*?"

Seeing how upset she was, Lena was torn between amusement and dismay. The girl had definitely changed. She couldn't imagine the person Sarah Jean once was daring to question anyone's decision. But she hadn't meant to worry her. She hadn't meant for her to know anything about this at all.

"Look, there's things they can do now," Sarah Jean said. "Medicine, chemotherapy—there's all kinds of stuff to fight cancer. You can't just give up and die, Lena. And if it's a question of money," she continued, "I'll get a job. I'll put the baby in daycare and I'll tell your doctor I'll give him money out of my pay. It's the least I can do for you, Lena," she said, her eyes filling with tears. "If you hadn't taken me in, I would have gone home and given up the baby and been miserable. Let me help you now."

Lena was touched, and it was a moment before she could speak. "No one's getting a job and putting Charlie in daycare," she said gruffly, clearing her throat. It had been years since anyone had made her cry. "I wasn't going to talk to anyone about this, but now that we've started, there's something else I might as well explain. While you were in the hospital, I made arrangements with my lawyer up north. I drew up a new will, leaving everything to you and Charlie. It's watertight," she added, thinking of Claire. "I said it was in consideration of the care you've given me in my last weeks."

"I don't want your money!" she burst out passionately but Lena held up her hand.

"Don't turn it down, child," she said, adding with a grin, "Actually, it isn't a bad bit of change. There's the savings account, of course. And you'll get my share of the house. You can sell it or keep it. I don't care which. And then there are a few CDs I bought. The certificates are in the safety deposit box at the bank."

Actually, more than a few. There would be plenty to keep Sarah Jean and Charlie safe, even if the pharmacist didn't come through with an offer of marriage.

Sarah Jean was silent. Lena relaxed back in the chair, tired from all the talk. It was getting harder each day to manage without taking all the pills she needed, but she had her own plans for them.

"I want a second opinion," Sarah Jean said finally with determination. "You're my responsibility now, Lena. I can't just let this go."

Lena looked at her with respect and a kind of relief. It appeared that it was no longer necessary for her to be the one in charge, to be looking out for their welfare. Sarah Jean was taking over, and Lena wasn't altogether unhappy with the idea. She needed the rest.

"I've seen other doctors," Lena said as gently as she could. "And they all proposed the same treatment but it wouldn't have changed the outcome. I just couldn't face it, child," and she shifted closer to her. It was suddenly very important that she understood, that she didn't think Lena was a coward taking the easy way out. Although, Lord knows, this way *wasn't* easy—not at all.

"All that stuff—that was one way, the way everybody said I had to do it. But they were all wearing blinders, Sarah Jean. There were other ways: to decide to die with some dignity and control. To leave the world all in one piece, not cut up and burned out. It's not that I want to die," she said earnestly. "But I kept seeing another way, and decided to take it instead. After all," she added sitting back, "we all have to die sometime."

"Lena," Sarah Jean began, but she waved her to silence once again.

"Anyway, about the money. There are only two stipulations. One is that you remember everything I've said about going through life with blinders on. Don't always choose the path that seems the safest or best, the one that everybody says you ought to pick. If I had done that, I'd be sitting in a hospital back home, and you'd still be hitchhiking on the interstate somewhere." She smiled at her to take away the sting of the words. "Follow your heart, and keep your eyes wide open. Use your peripheral vision, Sarah Jean. See the possibilities."

She nodded her head, and Lena continued.

"And when it comes time, Sarah Jean, I don't want anything special done for me. No tubes, no machines, no paddles flattening out this old lady's chest! I've already done the paperwork. Do you understand, Sarah Jean?" Lena grabbed her hands and held them tightly. "I'm relying on you to grant me this. It's my last request, child. Let me go my way."

Tears glistened on the young girl's cheeks, but she held onto Lena's hand, nodding her head. When she spoke, her voice was firm and certain.

"Whatever you want, Lena," and Lena knew it was a promise she would keep.

"All right, then," and Lena reached over to where the baby was starting to stir. It was time for Sarah Jean to nurse him. "Enough of this talking. It's time to feed your son."

Lena picked him up, ignoring the pain the movement caused her, and laid her cheek against his. Then, she handed him over.

"I'll just take a little rest while you feed him."

She leaned back, trying to breathe evenly despite the pain. Six months seemed very optimistic now. But it didn't matter. She was where she wanted to be with two people she loved more than she had ever loved anyone else.

In the distance, Lena could see the waves breaking and receding on the shore.

"The tide's going out," Sarah Jean murmured softly, looking out over the ocean. The fire of the sunlight was reflected in her clear eyes and turned the baby's curls to gold.

"Yes, I guess it is," Lena agreed, and then was silent as the pain washed over her. "Just let it go," and she closed her eyes.

About the Author

Nancy Christie has a passion for fiction, and has been making up stories since she was a child, engaging in "what if" and "let's pretend" activities that took her far beyond her northeastern Ohio home. Her short stories have appeared in print and online magazines, including *Ariel Chart*, *Two Cities Review*, *Streetlight Magazine*, *Talking River* and *The Chaffin Journal*, among others. Several of her stories have earned contest placement or awards.

For more information about Nancy Christie and her work, visit her website at www.nancychristie.com, read her writing blogs (One on One, The Writer's Place and Focus on Fiction) or follow her on social media: Twitter (@NChristie_OH), Facebook (@NancyChristieAuthor) and Goodreads (www.goodreads.com/NancyChristie).

About the Press

Unsolicited Press is a small press in Portland, Oregon. The team, a group of stalwart volunteers, produces stunning fiction, poetry, and creative nonfiction by established and emerging authors.

Learn more at unsolicitedpress.com.